GUARDING BRYNN

by

Florence Witkop

ISBN-13: 978-1-962168-56-4

CHAPTER 1

It was night and the storm outside was slowly building to a crescendo. The rain was getting worse, but I had to ignore it and think about what to do so I could deal with whatever had happened. Because it would be bad.

My father was never late. Ever. You could set your clock by his comings and goings. He should be there already and there was no place to stop between where he'd called and the cabin.

It was a ten-minute drive from the main road, and he'd called as he turned onto our gravel road. He'd asked me to get steaks out of the refrigerator. "Cell service will probably die so I called while I still could."

The family cabin was in an isolated area. Sometimes we had service, most of the time we didn't, and since my father loved steak, he'd wanted to make sure they were done right and since they were best if grilled at room temperature, he'd wanted me to get them out before he arrived. He'd almost apologized for calling. But he was hungry.

I'd heard a car about ten minutes after that call so at first I'd thought it was my father but it continued on past our cabin so it wasn't him. I'd waited ten more minutes, expecting his car to turn into the driveway. When that didn't happen, I became a bit uneasy. Another ten minutes and I was seriously concerned. After an additional ten I looked out the window and decided something had to be done. I got out boots, a poncho and a flashlight to go looking for him.

I'd need the gear. There was no moon, no stars because of the storm but I could still walk along the road. If I waited until the heart of the storm hit, the walk would be close to impossible and it would have to be a walk because he had the only car. Mine was in the city. But I knew the road. I could navigate it well enough even though it was night. The storm would make the darkness worse, of course. Pretty much like in horror stories.

I grabbed my rain gear and set off. Hopefully I'd meet him on the road and get the car seat wet when he gave me a ride back but he'd just roll his eyes and ask why I didn't wait a bit longer before getting all tied up in emotional knots and going out in a storm. Then he'd admit he was glad I did even though it wasn't necessary. He was that kind of father.

Never mind that he'd made a fortune and we were

richer than my parents had dreamed possible when they were first married and had got richer still as the years passed because he kept making money. Lots of money. But he was my dad and that was all that mattered at the moment. I couldn't bear the thought of anything happening to him.

I pointed the flashlight ahead as I walked, watching for headlights. Didn't happen. It was just a storm-tossed black night that grew even blacker as the worst of it hit with wind and rain that was a river of water falling from the sky.

When I reached an area where huge trees met overhead, the rain was less but the darkness was worse. It was so intense I could feel it. And still I saw no headlights and heard no car engine. Panic nibbled at the edges of my mind because I was almost at the highway.

Then I saw a dim glow ahead at the side of the road. I breathed a sigh of relief as I broke into a run because he'd clearly had engine trouble. We'd have to walk to the cabin and call for a tow truck, but we'd laugh about it afterwards.

Except, when I reached the car, it wasn't my father's. It was an older SUV with no one inside. I opened the door hoping to find out why it was empty and where my father was. The dome light lit up the surrounding area somewhat.

"Hey!" A voice cut through the dark and I backed out of the SUV and looked for the owner of the shout. "You, there! On the road. In the car."

"What?" I saw nothing through the rain that fell faster and harder with each passing minute. "Who's calling? I can't see you."

"Down here. He's hurt. I need help."

"Who's hurt?" But, with a sinking heart I knew who was hurt. My father. "Where are you?"

"At the bottom of the hill." I followed the voice and clambered and slid down the embankment on the side of the road and there, in the mud, was my father's car with someone pulling at the driver's side door trying to open it. It was crumpled and stuck. "Can you help? Maybe if we both pull it'll come open."

Together we pulled as hard as we could and slowly, with the metal protesting loudly, we got it open. "Dad!" I reached for him.

"Is he breathing?" The voice by my side was calm and collected.

I leaned as close as possible and put my ear to his chest. "Yes."

"Are you a nurse or a doctor?" I shook my head. "I'm not either but I've had some experience with trauma. Want me to take a look?"

I backed away and let him take my place, wrapping my arms around my waist as I started to shake. My father was hurt, and I couldn't see how bad but he wasn't speaking. He wasn't conscious.

"His pulse is strong and his breathing is normal." The man who'd found my father turned to me. "Can I use your flashlight?"

In the light my father looked normal except for a streak of blood across his forehead. And the fact that he wasn't conscious. "A concussion?" He pointed the beam lower. One leg was at an odd angle. "It's broken. If that's the worst that happened, he'll be okay. I don't know about the gash on his forehead, though."

My father moved. Opened his eyes and blinked in the bright light. He moved again and groaned. The man who'd found him said, "Take it easy. Don't try to move. We'll get you to a hospital." He turned back to me. "Call 911 and ask for an ambulance."

I tried and shook my head. "No cell service."

He swore. "Then we'll have to take him ourselves. That's my SUV on the side of the road but we have to get him up the hill and into it." He paused, finally seeing me now that the first phase of the emergency was past and there was time to think past the immediate moment. "You're his daughter, aren't you? I heard you call him 'Dad." I said I was, and he asked, "Can you do this? Can you do what needs to be done even if he cries out? It can be hard for a family member to see someone they love in pain."

"I can do whatever is needed." If I'd come upon my dad alone, I'd be doing everything myself. "And thank you for stopping." Then I asked what I hadn't thought about until then. "Do you know what happened?"

"I do." The voice that had been concerned turned grim. "He was run off the road by a driver that didn't stop and didn't render aid. He didn't even slow down. Just kept going."

"I heard a car pass a while back. That must have been it."

"Did you see it? The color? Anything that will identify it for the police?"

"Nothing. I only noticed because I was waiting for my dad and it came along at the right time."

My father groaned again and reached for me. "Brynn. Is that you?"

"It's me, Dad."

"I hurt. What happened?"

"You had an accident, but we'll get you to the hospital." How seriously was he hurt? How would we get him up the hill? I pushed a growing fear to the back of my mind and took his hand. "Don't worry, Dad. We'll take care of you."

He looked beyond me to the man who'd come along at the right time. "Who are you and can you help us?"

"I'm Jace Browne and it'll be a piece of cake, but we need your cooperation. We need to get you up the hill and into my SUV. Then you can sleep all the way to town."

My father nodded. "Okay." He looked around, willing himself to full consciousness bit by bit as seconds ticked away. "Tell me what to do."

"Your leg is broken. Before we do anything else, I want to splint it."

"I'm cold." My father shivered.

Jace Browne spoke low. "He's going to go into shock pretty soon, so we have to do this as quickly as possible. I'm going to the other side of the car to tend to his leg. You stay here and hold the flashlight." He examined me. "Can you do that?"

"I can do whatever I have to." I'd fall apart later.

"Good girl. Now I need something to wrap his leg with." He frowned. "Not his clothes. He needs them to stay warm." He started to pull his shirt off, but I stopped him.

"You're all wet. My shirt is dry under the poncho." I pulled my shirt off with the poncho still on to keep it dry and handed it over. He tore it into wide strips. "Is there anything to use as a splint? It should be splinted."

I'd tripped over small branches coming down the hill. Now I found one of the right length. He took the unused portion of my shirt to wipe it as dry as possible. Then he splinted my father's leg.

My father's eyes went wide with pain and he held my hand so hard the circulation was cut off. The resulting splint was clumsy but would keep his leg immobilized until a professional could look at it. Then we proceeded to get him out of the car.

I'd not have been able to do it alone. My father was a large man and I'm not large at all, but Jace Browne was as tall as my father, perhaps taller, and had an athletic build that spoke of sports or perhaps a military background and he took my father's full weight while I helped keep him steady. And slowly, carefully, inch by inch, we got him out of the car.

"Now for the hill. You just came down it. Do you know what it's like?"

"It's slippery. Really bad."

He swore under his breath, then took a firmer grip on my father who was shivering uncontrollably. "We have to get him warm soon." He looked at me through the rain. "Are you up to this? Can you take his other side and hold on if one of us slides?"

I nodded and we took the first step up the steep incline. The climb was three steps up and two steps sliding back with my father shaking harder as time passed while trying not to cry out in pain each time we slid backwards. I would have cried myself except we were too busy.

When I thought we were doomed to failure the road appeared and soon we were next to Jace Browne's SUV. "You open the passenger's door while I hold him."

"Shouldn't he be in the back seat so I can steady him?"

"He needs heat and it'll get warm faster in front." I nodded and soon my father was in the SUV. Jace Brown buckled him in and then got into the driver's side while I climbed in behind my father. Jace turned around in the middle of the road and we headed to town and the hospital as I prayed that my father would be okay until we got there.

As soon as we reached an area with cell service, I called the hospital and told them we were on our way. It was a short distance from there so there was no reason for them to send an ambulance and Jace Brown got us there as fast as any ambulance could have done and didn't cause another accident in the pouring rain which said something about his driving skills. The man could have been a race car driver and I was thankful he'd been nearby when my father's car was run off the road. But I put those thoughts aside as we pulled into the emergency entrance where people in medical garb were waiting with a gurney.

CHAPTER 2

"Thank you for everything," I told Jace Browne several hours later after the doctor said my father's leg was set and explained that he had a concussion but they didn't think it was serious enough to be kept overnight. So we were free to go. In the middle of the night. "I don't know what I'd have done without you."

I expected him to politely say I was welcome and leave. Instead, he looked at me through slitted eyes and asked, "How, exactly, do you plan on getting home?"

I sagged. "I don't know. I'll think of something."

"I'll take you."

I eyed the clock on the waiting room wall. "I can't ask you to stay longer. You've been here for hours." He hadn't complained or acted as if he was in a hurry. "You must be late for wherever you were headed."

His shoulders lifted. "No place, really, and no particular time to be there."

"You were going no place in a pouring rain?" I wanted to bite my tongue as soon as I spoke because my words were unthinking and too blunt. As usual. "I'm sorry. It's none of my business and I'm just glad you were there. But you've done so much already. I can't ask more."

"The motels in town are full. I know because I'd have stopped at one if there'd been a vacancy. That's why I kept going, rain or no rain." Which explained how he'd ended up on a country road in a thunderstorm in the middle of the night. "But it was no big deal. If I'd have slept in my car it wouldn't be the first time. But I'm here now, you don't have a way to get home, I happen to have a car and I'm at loose ends. So why not? Though a cup of coffee when we get there will be much appreciated."

I checked the clock again. It was past midnight Way past. "We have extra bedrooms. You're welcome to one of them. It's the least we can do."

"That would be wonderful. It's turning out to be a long night."

The downpour had lessened to an all-night rain by the time my father's paperwork was complete and a nurse wheeled him to the entrance. He was tired but alert and didn't complain as he was helped into the passenger seat of Jace's much-used SUV though the fact that he accepted help said how traumatic the accident had been. My father didn't let anyone help him. He'd spend his old age throwing things at nurses.

The ride home was quiet, with my father dozing and Jace driving as carefully as during the trip to the hospital but a lot slower. He knew how to get to where my father had been run off the road but needed directions after that. It was an easy couple more miles down the road but he'd have missed our driveway that was hidden by brush and evergreens. And, of course, there was the gate I had to open manually because the remote was in my father's car at the bottom of a ditch.

The gate was followed by the long driveway with numerous turns and twists that ran along a ridge that was acceptable in good weather and couldn't be navigated by even the best drivers when rain turned the ground into mud. But the rain hadn't yet turned it into a quagmire and Jace got us to the cabin.

I had to open the garage door manually for the same reason I'd had to open the gate, but the attached garage made getting my father into the house fairly easy. Soon he was in the living room and protesting that he wanted to enjoy coffee with Jace and me and there was no way we could force him to go to bed until he was good and ready. I figured the pain meds from the hospital were working.

So the three of us had strong, black coffee with tons of cream and sugar and a choice of flavors that turned simple coffee into luxurious treats until we were practically drowned in so much caffeine that we knew we'd not sleep a wink. We decided to stay awake and watch the sun come up if the rain ended and let it peek through. We did stay up till dawn by the clock but the rain never quit and we never saw sunshine. Eventually my father reluctantly agreed to go to bed.

I showed Jace a spare bedroom of the several my parents had insisted on being built when we had the cabin remodeled. He brought in a backpack containing his things and with no sun to wake us up because the rain still fell, we all three slept past noon.

Jace was already in the kitchen when I stumbled there after waking up. He was staring at the top-of-the-line cappuccino machine that took up half of one of the several kitchen counters from that remodel that my father had insisted would make cooking easier for my mother. Of course it didn't because she never cooked. She hated anything cooking related. But I loved the new kitchen. Now a frustrated Jace considered the cappuccino machine. "How does this thing work?"

"Darned if I know," my father said from the doorway as he appeared with the crutches he'd been given the night before but not used because he'd been too wiped out to even consider looking at them. But we'd brought them in and left them beside his bed.

Now he stared at his favorite nemesis, the cappuccino machine. "It's one of those ridiculous things that's so shiny it'll cause blindness if you look at it too long. It's supposed to do everything and more and it will if you can figure out how to use it which you can't because it's too complicated for normal minds to grasp its many functions so instead you use a real coffee pot to make actual coffee." He used a crutch to point at a cabinet door. "The one we used last night is in that cabinet."

Jace failed to hide a grin that he sent my way that said my father must be recovering nicely, judging by that speech and I grinned back. My father noticed and smiled along with us. Then he found the coffee pot we'd used since I was a kid and made coffee while I scrambled eggs and my father made toast, leaning his brand new crutches against the wall and smiling because, as he explained while the bread toasted, he was still here and kicking after having been in an accident. Plus the rain was ending, the sun was coming out, and life was good.

That sunshine, though, was brief. It lasted long enough for us to enjoy breakfast on the deck after wiping the furniture dry. It warmed our bodies nicely but shortly after bringing our dishes back inside a new batch of clouds scudded across the sky and turned the world dark once more. "Another storm already?"

My father frowned. "More rain means more mud. The driveway is already bad, another storm will make it deadly and the gravel road beyond the driveway will be every bit as bad. Both will be undriveable."

He looked at Jace. "I hope you don't have anywhere to be because you won't make it to the road, let alone to the highway, until the rain ends and the mud dries."

He waved expansively at the cabin that was now many times larger than when I'd been a kid, thanks to that remodel. "As you can see, we have a lot of room.

You're welcome to stay as long as you want, and I hope you do because I'd hate for you to die by mudslide after rescuing me and probably saving my life."

Jace's look met mine for the second time that day. He asked silently if my father meant what he was saying. I nodded imperceptibly that he did, indeed, mean every word as I promised myself that I'd explain further when we were alone. I'd explain how being able to offer things to people was a big deal to my father because he'd not been able to when he was growing up.

My father's eyes narrowed. He watched the private exchange between Jace and me and I knew he'd also noticed the first one a minute or so earlier. No the smile that had started when Jace and I communicated silently grew unexpectedly wider. Brighter. What's more he didn't try to hide that smile. We didn't need the sun because his smile was as bright as a sunny day.

Why'd two simple glances between Jace Browne and me almost set him dancing and would have if he'd had two good legs?

My father's eyes then slit in thought. He glanced at Jace Brown and inspected him covertly for a long time. Then his gaze moved to me for a split second. Then a look came over his face that no one would recognize except my mother and me and I only knew what he was thinking because I'd seen it many times during my life. It was the way he looked when he'd had a eureka moment. Those moments had always meant we'd be a bit richer than before.

The thing was, I knew this time his smile wasn't about money. It couldn't be because money hadn't been part of last night's misadventure. Instead, it had something to do with Jace. And possibly me because he'd looked at me after checking out Jace. So whatever my father was thinking had been triggered by the couple of looks between Jace and me.

What on earth was he thinking? More to the point, what was he planning because I knew for certain he was planning something and I had no idea what beyond that his thoughts were positive in nature and I only knew that because of that thousand watt smile.

My father watched Jace all that day and all day I could see his mind working overtime. I could read some of his thoughts, the ones he didn't try to conceal. He figured Jace had saved his life. Now he wanted to repay Jace and he'd do it his way, which meant he already had Jace's future planned out. That was how my father worked, engineering companies and people with equal aplomb, though just what kind of future he had in mind for Jace was more than I could guess.

Jace had already agreed to stay until it was safe to drive, a decision made after my father contacted a tow service to have his car towed and was told that, given the condition of the road, it couldn't be towed any time soon. Next week, maybe. Jace's eyes had gone wide and once again our looks had met as I'd indicated that, yes, our driveway and the road truly were that bad and my father wasn't exaggerating.

And once again, for a third time, my father noticed Jace and me communicating silently. And once again, he smiled and the smile had something to do with Jace and me because that look had only come over him when Jace and I communicated through covert looks.

The thing was, my father always had plans. They were his life's work and behind the several fortunes he'd made. I had no clue what this current plan might be, though, except that Jace was clearly special in my father's eyes and deserving of special treatment and my father was a generous man.

The thing was, Jace was an observant person. He knew my father was watching him, he just didn't know why. I didn't know either but decided that when my father wasn't present it would be my duty to explain my parent to the man who was now being considered for -- something.

That time came hours later as the sun would have slanted towards the treetops if the rain and clouds hadn't obscured it. My father finally, after much argument, had agreed to go back to bed. He was exhausted and needed sleep though he refused to admit it.

It was Jace who finally talked him into resting and my father only agreed because the man who'd saved his life and who he had plans for should be listened to so he'd be on Jace's good side in order to get Jace to do whatever he wanted him to do that caused that secret smile.

So he retired, leaving Jace and me to watch TV and the rain sluicing down the huge, floor-to-ceiling plate-glass windows that took the place of the more normal ones I'd grown up with.

"Nice place," Jace said cautiously as a beginning to a conversation.

"You can be honest, Jace. It's more than nice. It's huge, for starters, at least as cabins go. Spacious, I believe was the architect's term. And so well designed that all the money and work that went into the remodel isn't obvious. Which is good because I still love it even after it was remodeled almost out of existence."

He leaned against the back of his chair and chuckled. "Okay. I'll admit it. You said 'cabin' and that's what I expected so I was a bit surprised by this place when we arrived." His eyebrows drew together. "But not the driveway. It doesn't match the rest of the place. It's awful and I find that fact intriguing."

I laughed along with him but not so quietly. "When my father sold his first company, he immediately remodeled this cabin and money was no object. It's comfortable and convenient and has everything any of us could ever want. But he loves isolation and the driveway that we fought ever since I was tiny guarantees that we are isolated whether we want to be or not.

"My dad loves isolation. It gives him respite from working his ass off. He loves what he does but everyone needs a break, and this cabin forces him to rest a bit. So the driveway wasn't touched. As a result, I'm afraid you're stuck here until the mud dries."

CHAPTER 3

After that little speech, I turned to Jace. "Now you know about us. What about you?"

He shifted in his chair. "Like I said, I have nowhere in particular to go and no set schedule to get there."

"But you must have been going somewhere. Otherwise, why be going anywhere at all?"

"I'm recently discharged from the Army and have no plan for the rest of my life. I figured a trip might give me ideas."

"I suspect my father has ideas in that regard. Have you seen the way he watches you?"

"I noticed. Why? Does he think I'm a murderer or something?"

I tried to explain my father. "It's the way he is. How he works. He started a company when I was a tiny kid. Then he sold it and used the money to remodel the cabin and make more money. And so on. He hasn't stopped yet."

"So you are rich?"

"We live well."

"Obviously, but what's that got to do with him watching me?"

"I honestly don't know but when he looks at you, he has the same look he always has when he has a new, brilliant idea and his gut feelings about things are usually spot on. It's what has made him so successful."

He mulled that over. "I guess it doesn't matter why. I'll leave in a day or so."

"No you won't. I know this mud. With all the rain we've had it'll take a week for it to dry."

"Okay. So I'll stay more than a day or so. I'll enjoy every minute of my time here in this large and very comfortable so-called cabin."

At that moment my father's cell phone rang. I ran to get it because he was asleep but before I could reach his bedroom, I heard his voice. So I returned to the main room.

Minutes later my father showed up in his pajamas, leaning on those crutches and with the phone still in his hand. He stared at Jace. His face was unreadable except that happy look was gone, replaced by something totally serious. "You look military. Do you know how to handle a rifle?"

"Recent military so, yes, I know how to shoot."

My father's face turned even grimmer if such was possible. "Want a job?"

Jace examined my father and asked carefully and

with no expression whatsoever, "What kind of job?"

"The kind that might require using a weapon. I have rifles. They are for hunting but they work on the same principle as those you have experience with."

Jace didn't so much as blink. "What can you tell me about this job?"

"That was my wife on the phone. She says we are in danger. That someone is trying to do us harm."

Jace drew in his breath and expelled it slowly. "Like running you off the road."

My father nodded. "Like that. Or like kidnapping my daughter. There's been a threat. To my daughter, Brynn. To all of us, but to her specifically."

There was silence for a long time as my stomach turned over because someone wanted to harm me. And my family. All I heard was the ticking of the grandfather clock in a corner that had been there since long before the remodel until Jace asked quietly, "Did she say why someone might do that?"

"My wife is a biologist. An epidemiologist to be precise and she's in the Amazon now with a co-worker. They've made some cockamamy discovery I don't understand but evidently it's wonderful and someone wants it badly enough to have threatened her and her friend if they don't give them the formula." He grunted. "My wife doesn't take lightly to people doing that and she told them what they could do with their threat and where they could go."

"And shortly after she said that someone ran you

off the road."

My father nodded. "She's on her way home to explain but it'll take a while to get here."

"In the meantime, you have rifles here in the cabin and there are people for those rifles to protect. Your daughter, most of all." He looked around at the huge windows that could be easily broken by anyone who wanted to gain access. "And this place isn't a fortress. It's not very secure at all."

"Exactly. Interested?"

There was a pause of a half second before Jace replied. "Sure." He looked at me and our looks met. As had happened several times before. "Why not?"

My father nodded curtly as he noted that once more Jace and I had shared a private thought but this time he didn't smile. Instead his face showed anger at the situation we were in and relief that someone would help. "We'll discuss details in the morning. In the meantime, Brynn can show you where the gun cabinet is located and you can choose your weapon. Or weapons."

He turned toward his bedroom. He suddenly looked tired. Weary. Exhausted. As if the accident had finally got to him in spite of his insisting he was okay. He looked like he was on the verge of collapse. "Sleep with it next to you and make sure you are in the room next to Brynn."

He rubbed a hand across his face. "I hate to dump this in your lap with no more information, but I do need sleep. I'm afraid I'm not recovered completely yet."

"Go to bed. Get lots of sleep." Jace smiled without humor. "I'll take care of this place. I'll take care of your daughter."

"Thank you." My father nodded wearily. "Keep my daughter safe."

He started to his room, staggering with weariness and the news he'd just received, but before he took two steps Jace and I were beside him. Supporting him. Helping him. Making sure he got the rest he so badly needed because, yes, what had happened had caught up with him. Suddenly. Completely. When he was in bed we returned to the main room and sat for a long time taking in what we'd just been told.

I turned to Jace. "I, also, thank you."

"I wondered about your father being run off the road when it happened. It was deliberate, that was obvious. Now I know why it happened and I'd hate to see the idiot who did it finish what he started." He moved without seeming to. It was a subtle thing that rippled through his entire body and when he rose from his chair, he was somehow different. Taller. More sculpted. In charge.

That difference made me feel sorry for anyone who tried to mess with him. I decided I was glad Jace Browne had been around when my father was run off the road even though I couldn't quite wrap my mind around the idea that someone – anyone – would want to harm my family.

I rose until I stood beside him. Looked up at him because he was almost a head taller than me, a fact I'd not paid any attention to until strength and size were important. "I'll show you where the guns are kept." In a room behind the pantry that no one would know existed unless it was pointed out.

When I unlocked it with the key from a nearby shelf, Jace chose a thirty-thirty because he didn't need a long-range rifle in the forest surrounding the cabin nor in the cabin itself even if the worst happened and someone broke in. He looked for a pistol, but we didn't have any. Just hunting rifles, including a twenty-two for gophers.

He pointed to the twenty-two. "Do you know how to use that?" I did. I'd had a long-running dispute with gophers since just about forever. "Then that's the rifle for you." He made sure it was loaded and handed it to me. It was a light-weight rifle. It was comfortable. Jace smiled and led the way back to the main part of the cabin.

Then he moved his things into the room next to mine and insisted we both keep our doors open. I thought that particular precaution was over the top but didn't say anything. His actions said he knew his job and his body language said it wouldn't do any good to argue. Not to mention that he was now in charge of security, which meant that at least for the near future he was in charge of me.

As I stared at the ceiling that night and failed to

sleep because who could sleep after having their life threatened, I wondered if a job in security was what my father had been considering for Jace all along. The reason for those speculative looks. Of course he hadn't known about the threat when that lightbulb expression first crossed his face the first time Jace and I shared a look. But Jace knew what to do in a dicey situation, such as a roadside emergency, so security might have been what he was considering and all businesses need security and my father had several businesses.

The next day both Jace and my father spent a fair amount of time on the phone with the police because my father had been too tired to go through more stress by going to the police station in the middle of the night after being released from the hospital and, of course, with neither the driveway nor the road useable, they now had no way of getting there later. Hence the phone call instead of an in-person visit.

My father hadn't seen the car or its occupant and Jace hadn't got a good enough look at the license plate to be helpful beyond that the car was a dark color. Probably red or black. Not enough information to enable the law to find it. So my father was inclined to forget it. He would have brushed it off as an exercise in futility. "Whoever did it is gone. No sense doing anything now. I shouldn't have bothered the police."

Jace saw it differently. "If it's on record now, then if something else happens the authorities are more likely to take the new threat seriously." We were in the cabin's main room. At Jace's words, my father's face lit up still again in an expression that said he'd made the right decision asking Jace's help for protection because Jace obviously knew more about such situations than he did.

When the call ended there was silence in the room. I asked, "What next?" Because my father's tacit acceptance of Jace's expertise and lack of further questions said as loudly as a shout that he completely trusted the third person in the cabin, not to mention which the silence was deafening.

Jace grinned. "We wait for the rain to end and the mud to dry." As if that was what I'd asked about, though he knew I really wanted to talk about the threat to our lives.

I pointed to the world beyond the windows where a steady downpour said a dry driveway would be a long time in the future. "What do we do until then? With bad people possibly looking for us?"

My father's eyes slitted. Then he slumped ever so slightly. "I'm afraid I'm still tired. I need rest." He turned to me with an apologetic look that was so phony no one with an iota of sense would think it was real. After almost collapsing earlier and sleeping just about forever he definitely was not tired. But for some reason he wanted out of being sociable.

"I'm afraid what happens now is up to you two. You guys wait and be safe. Both of you. Do whatever you two decide to do." He went silent for a few seconds before continuing. "I'm tired so it's up to you entertain our guest, Brynn, and get him acquainted with the layout of the place or whatever else he needs to know while I recover from my recent ordeal."

He turned to Jace. "As for you, Jace, you are now a man with a job and don't you forget it. Protect my daughter." And he thumped on crutches to his room where I was fairly sure he spent the rest of the morning reading or catching up on work because he hadn't gone there to sleep because he wasn't tired. No, whatever had made him disappear had something to do with what he wanted from Jace though why he was giving Jace and me privacy was more than I could figure out.

But my father had given me hostess duty. I eyed the competent man before me and tried to think what would interest an uber male guy. We were in the main room and the silence was growing louder with each passing minute. I'd always hated being a hostess because I didn't know what to do. Never had, plus the fact that Jace was definitely a competent, alpha male and his type hadn't been part of my life until then so I didn't know anything about such guys, which made being hostess that much more difficult.

Lately the only guys I'd met either had tons of money and thought we belonged together because I also came from money, or they wanted to marry me because my father had money and I was an only child and they figured if they married me they'd get some of it.

I wasn't interested in any of them though they

seemed to be the only type of guy I'd met since our family became uber rich. Hence my visit to the cabin for peace and quiet and a little sanity.

Fortunately, my job crunching numbers for a number-crunching company could be done by anyone, so I'd been given leave of absence without an argument. They had lots of number crunchers. Losing one temporarily wasn't a big deal.

So, as I stared at the rain beyond the window and the man beside me, I could concentrate solely on entertaining one very uber male guy. Except I didn't know what to do. As it turned out, though, Jace's military experience had instilled the habit of keeping weapons ready for action so, after giving me a look that said he knew I was struggling with what to do next, he suggested we return to the gun cabinet.

"Do you have cleaning kits for the rifles, and do they need cleaning?" It was a polite question asked as I stared at him awkwardly and wondered what to do next.

"On the top shelf and I can't remember the last time they were cleaned."

So he spent the better part of the day cleaning rifles with me watching. I wondered how hard my father would laugh at that unusual result of my failure to play the charming hostess, a role I'd never mastered. He always found my lack of social skills amusing because they came so easily to him.

As Jace cleaned rifles and the rain sluiced down the windows and turned dirt into mud and the sun stayed hidden from view and I covertly inspected him, I found him more and still more interesting. I wished I could see into his mind because the more I watched the more intrigued I became by this former military man who seemed comfortable anywhere, even in our cabin that had been remodeled into what could be described as opulent.

And the more intrigued I was the more I noticed him as a man. Sculpted. Tall. Quiet like a panther. Deliberate. Relaxed. The kind of man I'd have spent my life waiting to fall in lust with if I'd realized such men existed. Which I hadn't until he came along.

CHAPTER 4

The rain ended. The sun came out and dried up everything except the muddy driveway and the equally muddy road. Thankfully, Jace no longer cared that he couldn't leave because he now had a place to be and a job.

The road became drivable before the driveway did. Enough that a tow truck could get through, though with great difficulty. My father's car was towed to the repair shop before we even dared step off the porch and into the muddy mess we called a yard that had never known a lawnmower or flower garden or any other of the usual civilized amenities.

When we did take that first step off the deck, Jace and I stepped gingerly so as not to end up slipping and taking a mud bath while my father remained on the porch because he'd have surely taken a dive with his crutches.

But it was clear how much he loved the whole sloppy mess of a yard that contrasted so totally with his city life as a businessman complete with suits and ties. He took a deep breath and smiled broadly as Jace and I made our careful way through the mud.

As we moved through the yard, he called out his appreciation that the guns were cleaned and his expression said it was the kind of thing he'd expected from a man like Jace.

Then he changed the subject.

He began with a simple statement as he stood on the deck and regarded Jace and me in the middle of the muddy driveway. "I'm glad you two made sure the guns are ready to be used if needed." I waited because it wasn't a simple statement. I knew his tone of voice. There was more.

His next words explained everything. "Because a while ago I got another call from Abigail." He looked at Jace who didn't know who Abigail was. "My wife."

Jace and I made our way to the relatively safe area of the small patio that had been there forever and hadn't been changed when the cabin was remodeled even though it served no purpose beyond looking quaint. As we surveyed the surrounding yard and forest from the safety of the patio, Jace looked a question at my father. "I'm guessing you're telling us about the call from your wife because it was important."

"My wife and her co-worker were forced off the road."

Jace nodded calmly while I went into an emotional tailspin. "Was she the targeted victim? What do you know about the co-worker?"

"Russell Manners. A crusty guy who's old enough to be her grandfather but he refuses to retire." Said with admiration because my father would never retire either as I mentally pictured the white-haired eccentric my mother often partnered with in her search for new drugs that took the two of them all over the world. "I can't imagine anyone believing he's worth targeting even though he's as sharp as a tack. He doesn't look or act competent even though he is."

Jace asked a question. "So you think the target was your wife?" My father nodded. "Which means two members of your family have been attacked in the space of a few days." Jace's eyes slitted and his voice was deceptively calm.

"I have no doubt about it and I hope she gets home soon so I can find out what she and Russell are up to that's so important that people are going to such extremes to get it for themselves."

My father moved to the edge of the porch with the help of his crutches and eyed the yard with the aim of joining us on the patio. We quickly returned to the deck before he could try.

"So, Jace, I'm glad you are here and I'm glad the weather conspired to keep you here because there's something I wish to talk to you about that I've been considering for a while but that Abigail's call made even more imperative. Something a bit more than what you are already doing." Jace waited for him to continue, arms crossed, body relaxed and totally alert. "I have a deal for you if you are interested. And I hope you are."

Jace cocked his head. "What kind of deal?"

"I asked you to protect my daughter after the first call from Abigail. And you agreed. No questions, no hesitation. You just took on the challenge." My father took a deep breath and considered the man who'd come into our lives in such an unusual way. "What to make it a real job with pay and benefits that will last as long as you agree to work for me? Permanent if you choose?"

He continued, his voice full of anger. "The only reason Brynn wasn't run off the road like Abigail and I were is because she was here in the cabin. But she's my only child and she'll be the next victim if the opportunity arises. Whoever did this made sure we know she's the preferred target."

His eyes were smoke and fire. "No one messes with my kid. But just because I'm her father doesn't mean I can do the best job of protecting her. And I don't know when she'll be safe even when this is over with. Or if she'll ever be safe. I have a lot of money and there will always be people who want it and they clearly are willing to go after her in order to get some of it. Her safety is something I never had to think about until lately but I'm thinking of it now. I want to know she's safe from this problem and then I want to keep her safe permanently."

He stopped for a moment and his nostrils flared as his hands gripped his crutches as hard as possible and he stared at Jace. Hard. "I want you to keep Brynn safe, Jase. You. No one else. You. Jace Browne. You are the person I want to do this for me because I believe you are the best man for the job and I know you'll do it right. Furthermore, I'd like you to do it for as long as needed and that could be a long time considering how much money I'm worth. Years perhaps or forever." He paused, then asked, "Interested?"

Jace didn't answer immediately. He looked at my father for a long while, taking stock of the man who'd just offered him a job few people would choose. Then his look shifted to me, but I had no idea what he was thinking as that look went from the top of my head to my toes and took in everything in between.

I felt that look in every atom of my being, but it wasn't an unpleasant sensation. In fact, it was quite – nice. But his look gave away nothing of his thoughts.

"Okay." He said one word and my father relaxed while Jace remained the same enigmatic person who'd just examined every bit of me. As for me, I managed not to shake from having been inspected and/or considered by two men for the same reason but in completely different ways. The fatherly way and the Jace way, whatever that was.

My father clapped his hands. "So that's settled. Later on, we can work out the details. Right now, let's celebrate. I have some wine somewhere and I'm tired of thinking bad thoughts. What say we have some wine and consider the world." Then he grinned wickedly. "I love celebrations and this will be one of the best because I got what I badly needed, which is someone who'll keep my daughter safe."

"And Mom's on her way home," I pointed out, knowing how prized animals must feel as they are inspected on the auction block. Not an accurate comparison but similar enough. I'd been discussed and examined as if I was a rare and valuable commodity. "Another reason to celebrate."

My father nodded. "I miss your mother when she's in the middle of some remote jungle or wherever she thinks the next big drug will be discovered." He led the way inside where I found a bottle of wine in the back of a kitchen cabinet because the remodel hadn't included a wine cellar even though the architect had suggested we have one because people of our status always did. That alone had made my father refuse to have one because he hated status symbols. So it was up to me to locate the wine for our impromptu celebration.

It was the only bottle we had so I hoped it was the right wine for the time of day or kind of celebration or whatever reason people who knew wine would say was appropriate or else I hoped that Jase wouldn't know the difference any more than I did. I took the bottle and turned to go back to the porch.

Jase stood in the doorway to the pantry, leaning against it and watching me. "Are you okay with this plan of your dad's?" He watched me much as when he'd done his head-to-toe examination but slower and more subtly. "I noticed he didn't ask you if you want someone protecting you. Or if you want me to be that someone."

I hugged the wine. "I'm okay with it."

"I believe it's the right thing to do considering what's been going on and your father's business success. One of your family being attacked is bad. Two of you takes it to a whole different level of danger. Most importantly, though, is the fact that you were threatened specifically. Just you."

"Do you really think it's that bad?"

He nodded. "Think about it. What happened was deliberate. More than that, it was coordinated in more than one country. Consider the organization required." He levered himself from the doorway and led the way through the kitchen and back towards the porch. "So, yes, I believe a very high level of concern is warranted."

We never reached the porch because my father was in the living room on the couch, leaning against the back with his eyes closed. He looked weary. Exhausted. And he was asleep. I suddenly realized how hard he'd been pushing himself since his accident, not relaxing until now. Until his daughter was safe because he'd arranged it. I felt guilty for being the cause of such concern.

I turned away from Jace so he'd not see my sudden tears, but it was too late. He gently took the bottle of wine and placed it on the coffee table. Then he simply pulled me against his chest and said, "It'll be okay. Someday this will all blow over. I promise. In the meantime, you can cry if you want." Then, with a slight lilt to his voice. "Your father is asleep, so he won't notice."

That last comment made me giggle quietly against his chest because in the days since meeting my father, Jace had somehow managed to figure out what made him tick and that my father saw me as a delicate daughter who needed protection. Forget that I was a normal, competent, American female who didn't take any BS from anyone, he was my dad and dads protect their daughters. Mostly, though, he'd figured out that my father noticed everything and paid particular attention whenever Jace and I communicated silently. Or smiled at the same time. Or laughed together. Or anything at all. He noticed. Every. Single. Time.

But Jace's chest felt good. So good. So I lingered and reveled in the feel of him. The warmth of him. The safety he exuded as easily as he breathed. As easily as he gave off something else. A vibe that was totally male and very potent.

After a moment against a warm, hard chest, though, I pulled away and retrieved the wine from the coffee table and found some glasses so when my father awoke we could have some. I also found some strawberries and chocolate and Jace didn't comment on whether we had the proper wine for our celebration or not.

As my father slept, Jace and I drank coffee in order to save the wine for later. Seeing his long legs awkwardly sticking out in front of him I put mine on the coffee table to let him know feet on furniture was acceptable and soon his also were stretched out.

He was thinking. "It's not just you, Brynn. Your entire family is in danger." I could see in his face that he was thinking through this new, odd job he'd just accepted. Not just me, he was accepting responsibility for all of us. "Tell me about your mother," he finally said. "Since she seems to be the catalyst in this situation."

"She's both a medical doctor and a biologist," I said by way of explanation. "An internist and a biologist but her true calling is searching out and finding new medicines for the things that current drugs don't work well for." I went silent as I remembered a childhood with a mother who was always torn between her family and her need to find a cure for still another ailment.

"That's where Russell Manners comes in. Russell has been doing what my mother wanted to do forever but he's never been good at finding financing. My father has done well financially, and my mother is just as passionate as Russell about finding new drugs. So it's a natural partnership. My dad funds their trips and they split the profit of anything that turns out to be useful." I laughed. "But the lag between finding a drug and getting it to market is so long that profit hasn't yet happened."

"I'm guessing your father doesn't care about the cost as long as your mother is happy and she and this Russell person are doing good things?"

"That's right."

"He cares about things that matter to him. His family."

Which made me remember the wine we were supposed to be using to celebrate still being an intact family. "Is the wine the right kind? It's all we have."

He moved his feet enough to examine the bottle of wine on the table. "It's in a bottle, not a cardboard box. That's high end as far as I'm concerned."

I laughed. I couldn't help it. No matter that my parents had both been attacked and I'd been threatened, it felt good to laugh. Jace soon joined in though we kept it quiet so as not to wake my father.

That laugh made me realize I was glad Jace would be around for the foreseeable future and possibly forever. And not just because he knew how to use a firearm. Because he made me feel safe. And good. And because he made me laugh.

CHAPTER 5

As I laughed, I realized how important Jace had become in such a short time. I could laugh because of him. I could feel safe because he was near. But what about Jace himself? I felt guilty for not thinking of him and decided to remedy that situation. "You said you had no place to be and no particular time to be there. Was that true? Or are you giving up something and not telling us?"

He slanted a look my way. "I'm not giving up anything beyond a little of my time."

"Are you sure about that?" I stared at him. Hard. Dared him to prevaricate.

"Life will happen and I'm okay with however it works out in the near future or long term." He looked comfortable with his decision to go to work for my father. But you never know about things like that so I asked the big question. The one that mattered. "Are you choosing to do this because it works for you or has my father hypnotized you?" I loved my father. But I knew him.

He laughed. Again. But this time he threw back his head and gave a deep, baritone belly laugh. "No, he has not hypnotized me, although after meeting him I can understand why you asked. I suspect he usually gets what he wants." That belly laugh said that, yes, Jace was telling the truth. And that he, too, had my father figured out.

I exhaled a long, relieved sigh. "I'm forever grateful that his wants are for good things. I shudder to think what the world would be like if he was a Mafia boss."

At that moment my father woke up, rested and looking like he was truly on the road to recovery. I hoped he hadn't heard us talking about him. He probably had. But he said nothing and acted innocent as a babe. "Your mother called while you were getting the wine. She's left the Amazon and is on her way here."

"Will the driveway be usable by the time she arrives?"

"If not I promised we'll meet her at the road with the four-wheeler." It would be a dicey trip, but it was possible. "She's been gone a long time and wants to be home, driveway or not." He wanted her home as badly as she wanted to be there.

"Is Russell with her?"

He shook his head. "Russell wants to do some research on the new drug. He needs a laboratory. Don't know what it's about but I suspect we'll find out when Abagail gets here." He included Jace in the conversation. "You'll like Abagail. She's one great researcher and can talk your arm and leg off about obscure diseases and the wonder drugs that cure them and the weird parts of the world where she finds those unique and very special drugs." As an afterthought, he added, "People say Russell is the senior partner, but I know my Abagail."

I caught Jace's attention, and he got the idea. Yes, my mother was bright, perhaps even gifted, and a hard worker but Russell was a legend in the business of finding new wonder drugs.

Two days later my mother arrived during that brief but confusing moment between when night ended and dawn broke and, yes, she left her car on the road because the driveway was still a muddy mess. She was brought to the cabin via the four-wheeler with Jace driving because my father had a broken leg and wouldn't allow me to pick her up because that could 'expose me to danger.' I chafed but accepted his decision because Jace agreed with him and not for any other reason.

Once she was in the house, she rested a bit, dragged her worn, frayed, sand-and-dirt-encrusted luggage into the master bedroom, fretted over my father's broken leg, said the driveway needed to be rebuilt, accepted my father's wish for it to remain the muddy disaster he so loved, and told us she'd been followed on her way to the cabin by people who tried to do her harm. Run her off the road at the very least.

Maybe worse.

It took a moment for me to process that last bit. "That's twice someone tried to run you off the road and once Dad was run off."

Jace, with the look I'd come to recognize that said he was thinking, asked, "Did you get the license number? Can you identify the car?"

My mother shook her head that, no, she couldn't help identify the car as my father fumed. "Whatever you and Russell discovered in whichever of the several countries you were in that had whatever it was you were looking for must be a whole lot more important than any of us imagined."

My mother sank into the soft cushions of the couch and gave a sigh of contentment. "It's good to be home." My father glowered at no one in particular as he waited impatiently to learn why we were in danger. Finally she turned to him and looked him up and down. "And to answer your unasked question, I believe what we discovered might be important. Hugely important. Maybe."

"Is that what Russell is checking out in some laboratory?"

"Yes, and he's doing it in a laboratory that was funded by you, Gaylord, so he has expedited access and will be working as fast as possible." She sipped the tea I'd made in honor of her return and closed her eyes in ecstasy. My mother loved exotic tea. "But it'll be a while before we know the truth because the research is slow, and the results can't be rushed. Unfortunately."

My father's body vibrated with tension. "So what is this discovery that's so important? Are you going to tell us?"

Her eyes opened. She examined us as we stared at her. She put her tea down. "It's a drug that appears to provide immunity that's so enhanced that the people where it's found seldom get any kind of infection at all. The statistics are clear. They almost never catch infectious diseases."

"So they never die?"

"They die from accidents. Of old age. Of inherited conditions. Of anything and everything people can die from, but they almost never die from an illness caused by an infection. It happens now and then but the numbers are statistically insignificant and happen just often enough that nothing was noticed until we started digging."

She retrieved her tea and took another sip as we waited for her to finish because she clearly wasn't done. "No red flags ever went up because people there die from viruses. Fungi. All the usual things. But when Russell and I dug into the statistics, the lack of deaths due to infections of any kind was remarkable."

"So you investigated."

"It's what we do and we believe this time we hit the jackpot. We hope so. Think what it can mean if we are right. It's a very wide spectrum immunity drug that's incredibly effective and since it's for immunity, not to cure something, there's no reason to think bacteria will become resistant to it. Ever." She paused a moment. "That's what we think, anyway. Russell will find out for sure."

"So we're being targeted because you're doing a good thing? A wonderful thing? Why would anyone do that?"

My father snorted. "Because it's also a wonderful thing for the bank account of whomever gets it to market first, and someone wants to make sure that isn't yours truly."

Jace continued with that line of thought. "Which means running you off the road was just a first step. If that first threat convinces you to fork over the formula, then nothing more will happen. If it doesn't and you take the first baby steps to get the drug on the market, they'll up the ante and do whatever they need to do to get what they want. To get it for themselves. To keep it off the market until they can steal it and get it there first." He was silent for a second. We all were. "Because the financial rewards will be huge enough to do whatever it takes to get you out of the picture."

My father's arm went unconsciously around my mother and his eyes focused on me. We were his family. I saw it in the sudden set of his jaw that said no one would harm us if he had anything to say about it, but that look also said he was too stubborn to give in to terrorist tactics. His and Jace's looks met and something passed between them that I couldn't read.

My mother finished her tea. "Which is why I think I was followed just now."

We stopped breathing for a moment. Her statement was that unexpected. "Could it have been your imagination? After all that's happened lately, I'd be suspicious of every vehicle on the road."

"I can't be sure, of course, but I think I was. They came up behind me fast and I think they were about to force me off the road when I turned onto the driveway. It's a mud bath as usual after a rain. I think they were surprised by that and when the driver saw the mud, he swerved in order to avoid sliding all over the place. Once he was straight again, he got back on the road and disappeared fast."

Jace rose calmly. "I'll check it out."

"Will you be able to tell?"

He shrugged. "It's a rural road and not well maintained. Not pavement though it's not total mud like the driveway. But it's still not dry so tracks might show." He paused. "But I should get out there while they are still fresh. If they are there at all. Which I suspect they are and that they will tell an interesting story."

"I'm going with you." I joined him.

My mother started to protest but my father saw my determined expression and shook his head ever so slightly at her and she subsided though it was clear she wasn't happy.

My father said, "Stay with Jace. Do not wander."

The protect-my-daughter-at-all-costs thing again. "I can take care of myself."

"You have no experience with people like the ones we are dealing with. Jace is former military and I suspect he's had other experiences that taught him a lot. So listen to him." Then he added, with a small wave of his free hand and an expression that said I'd inherited my stubbornness from him and he knew I'd do whatever I chose no matter his orders. "Please."

We took both four-wheelers. I followed in Jace's tracks and we got to the end of the driveway without incident. My mother's car was parked to one side where it would remain until the driveway was decent.

Then we checked for tire tracks. I was glad Jace was there to validate what I saw. It was fairly easy to read the tracks and know what happened, but I felt a need to say it out loud. "She was right about what happened."

He nodded and pointed to the tracks we were examining. "The second vehicle started to turn into the driveway. It was going faster than was safe, probably because the driver didn't expect mud. When he saw what the driveway was like he slammed on his brakes." The tracks showed where the vehicle had slid sidewise and almost gone over a small cliff. "The cliff scared him. He didn't want to end up at the bottom of a ravine, so he slowly and carefully backed away, turned around, and left."

"Can you know for sure that's what happened?"

"Not from the tracks alone. But together with what your mother said, it's pretty clear." He moved towards his four-wheeler because the inspection was done. "If whoever was in the car following your mother was a friend, he'd have called out to tell her he'd come some other time when it wasn't muddy. But he didn't."

"So someone really is out to get us." The last tiny doubt was erased.

"It's worse than just that, I'm afraid. So many attacks in such a short time means it's beyond serious." Chilling words that didn't speak well for the future and Jace didn't say just how bad 'beyond serious' was.

As we returned to the cabin, I changed my mind about the driveway. Maybe it wasn't a ridiculous affectation of my father's after all. Maybe it was a safety feature like the moats that protected castles of old.

CHAPTER 6

My mother was napping when we returned, tired after a long and draining flight followed by the drive to the cabin. My father was reading, his glasses pushed up as usual. Everything looked so normal I wanted to scream.

Jace seemed to sense how I felt. He reached out and squeezed my hand. I relaxed and was about to say something when the phone rang. It was the land line, which meant it was someone we knew because we told few people about the land line. It was a kind of guarantee of privacy in a place with dicey cell service.

My mother flew out of her bedroom, nap forgotten and answered. "It's Russell." Which meant she'd been expecting his call. She answered the phone, tiredness forgotten, and settled into an easy chair. It was going to be a long conversation. My father, Jace, and I also settled down and waited. It was a long wait, listening to one-word answers to whatever Russell was saying and shifting uncomfortably because those monosyllabic answers told us nothing.

Eventually she put down the phone and turned to us. "Well that settles it. I doubt we have to wait for the test results. The grapevine has told us all we need to know. The test results will merely provide proof."

My father removed his glasses so he could see her better. "Which is what, exactly?"

"That the drug I told you about does indeed provide immunity to a vast spectrum of infections." There was pride of a job well done in her voice.

"Would you care to explain further? Just a while ago you said it would take time to get any results."

"According to Russell, when he arrived at the research facility he learned the news of our discovery is all over the pharmaceutical business. Everyone is talking about it and gossip in the pharmaceutical field is usually spot on as far as technicalities are concerned. If someone got even a hint of what we have and how it works, they'd have made the technical connections and come up with the correct conclusion."

"If that's so then the attacks on us make no sense. No reason to attack us if everyone already knows everything."

"They don't know everything, that's what Russell called to tell me. They don't know enough to replicate what we found. Everyone is trying to find out the details and no one even knows who to ask. They are asking each other where it can be found, what it actually is, what it will do, and if it's as good as everyone thinks." She spread her hands. "They are rushing around like a bunch of chickens because no one knows anything beyond the rumors and that where there's smoke there's probably fire so the whole pharmaceutical field is going crazy. But the researchers punched in the numbers and say it should work. They just need to be filled in on the details. We have those details and they don't."

"Has anyone questioned Russell?"

She shook her head. "No because they don't know he can tell them anything. That's what a lot of the speculation out there is about. Everyone is asking everyone else who found it. Who to talk to. Who can answer questions. Who knows the details."

"Then why are we being attacked if no one knows you and Russell made the discovery?"

"Someone obviously knows."

Jace spoke for the first time. "I believe that explains why they tried to run you off the road instead of something more serious. An attack on your lives would be serious enough to alert the authorities. It could be traced back to them as being the people who knew enough to know who to hurt. The police are very good at back-tracking."

He thought a moment and then added, "They figure if they scare you enough times by running you off the road or whatever other tactics they dream up that won't call serious attention to them that you'll eventually give up. Then they'll come in and figure out what you found, where you found it, head over to the originators of the drug, and scoop up the prize."

"Does that mean they aren't out to hurt us?"

Jace shook his head. "I'm afraid not. You're on the cusp of something big and if time is important then they must hurry." He looked slightly apologetic as he continued. "They might very well decide to take out one of the two partners in order to send a message to the other to give them the formula. They'll make it look like an accident but the other partner will know the truth and hopefully be scared into giving them the information they need to acquire the drug for themselves. If that partner wants to stay alive."

We absorbed his words. Then I asked, "Does that mean Russell is the one in the most danger because he's not safe in a cabin in the woods?"

Jace nodded imperceptibly. "Whomever is the easiest to get to is in the most danger."

My mother picked up the phone. "I've got to call him. Warn him."

My father spoke. "Tell him to come here. It's the safest place."

"Think he'll be run off the road on the way? He's old and there are hours of driving to get here. His driving is adequate but he's not up to evasive maneuvers."

My father looked at Jace. "Does your driving match your other skills? Can you get him here even if someone tries to stop you?"

Jace's expression didn't change. "Probably. But no one is perfect."

"Go get him if you think you can get him here alive." Jace nodded his acceptance. "I'll stay on guard twenty-four seven with a rifle until you return."

Then my father said something odd and his eyes lit up in a way similar to when he'd first met Jace. After the accident. When he was considering Jace for something. "When you return, we'll talk. That talk I promised a while ago that we somehow never got around to. The details of your job. The important stuff." The stuff that would keep Jace employed by my father for as long as he wanted.

Jace nodded a second time and I couldn't believe how good his response made me feel. I didn't know why, didn't even try to explore the reasons because they were all mixed up and beyond analyzing. Perhaps danger did that. It messed up emotions and reasons until you couldn't tell one feeling from another or how you should think. And with all that had happened I was definitely messed up.

My mother picked up the phone to call Russell but Jace motioned for her to wait. "There's one more thing. You should file a police report on this morning's incident and I suspect it'll involve the police going to the road and checking it out. Since the driveway is such a mess maybe you'd prefer that I handle the transportation to talk to them before heading out to pick up this Russell person. We can go to town in your car. It's parked at the end of the driveway. We can talk to the police in person and file a report."

My parents nodded. "We should go now in case they want to check out the tracks. Before they degrade."

We headed for my mother's car in the four-wheelers. Then we continued on in her car. After a couple hours talking to an officer in a room we all managed to crowd into, they did, indeed, choose to examine the tire tracks after listening to my parents' explanation of all that had happened recently. The elderly officer who listened politely but intently said, "Being run off the road twice is enough to be concerning and an emergency room visit and broken leg can't be ignored." He carefully read the report of my father being run off the road he and Jace had called in.

Then he led us to an outer room where a second officer sat at a desk. Possibly the two of them made up the entire police force for the tiny town. "I'm heading out to look at the tracks, Tom," he told that officer.

"Take a few pictures. See what they tell me."

So we all returned to the driveway. He examined the tracks and took pictures from several angles. He gazed at the driveway with an expression that said if it was his, it would be usable instead of a muddy morass. Then he turned to my mother. "Are you sure you can't identify the car or driver?"

"It was too early to see clearly and I was too busy not sliding down the embankment to pay attention to the driver." She pointed apologetically to the tracks. "That's all the evidence there is."

"We'll check the tracks against known tire treads. Maybe something will jump out at us." He put his phone back in his pocket. "But don't get too excited because they'll most likely be the most common tires on the market. They usually are if it's a professional job and this sounds like a pro because they tried at least twice." He checked the tracks one more time. "Or this could truly be a random occurrence. Someone who thought the driveway was a road and left as soon as he saw it wasn't. I don't think that's the case but we can't rule it out."

How hard would he work comparing the pictures of tracks with known tire treads if there was a possibility it was a coincidence? I felt a sinking sensation as I wondered if the police force truly did consist of just two men. If so, how much time did they have to allocate to a crime that might not actually be a crime?

He returned to town and we returned to the cabin the same way we left, leaving my mother's car at the entrance to the driveway. One at a time on the four-wheeler with Jace driving.

"But the driveway is drying up nicely. It'll be useable fairly soon."

My mother rubbed a hand across her eyes. She was tired with a weariness that went beyond needing a night's sleep. "Tomorrow Russell will be here with his car beside mine at the road and Jace bringing him here in the four-wheeler. Then we'll be able to make some decisions."

My father started to pace, crutches thumping loudly as he sorted his thoughts. "This situation is bigger than us and requires major plans. It's clear we can't count on a small police force in a small town. First because of the enormity of your discovery, the help it will be to mankind. Second because the safety of my family is my responsibility and that tiny police force isn't enough." He frowned and stopped in the middle of the room. "This whole wonderful drug thing has changed from being good for all mankind in a general kind of way. It's personal now."

He returned to pacing and his steps speeded up in tandem with his thoughts, the thumping louder as his anger rose. "Since offense is the best defense I suggest we go on the offence." He stopped, looked to Jace for confirmation, and when Jace didn't argue, he continued both his pacing and his developing ideas. "To do so, we need a viable strategy."

He stopped again and looked at my mother, the person who, along with her partner, had discovered the drug. "Which is why Russell has to be here. Because he's involved and must help make decisions. And to keep him alive because, judging by what's happened so far, that's in doubt if he remains where he is."

My mother called Russell and told him what was

going on. After agreeing to come to the cabin, he had more news of his own. My mother passed it on to us. "More had happened since our last conversation."

She and Russell talked for quite a while and when they were done my mother took a deep breath and said things had changed. "The entire pharmaceutical world now knows Russell and I are the people who found the drug."

"How'd that happen?"

"Not that many people scour the world looking for new drugs. Unscrupulous people regularly follow all such researchers in the hopes of scooping our discoveries. Even totally honest drug companies aren't above listening to the gossip and then putting what they hear together with their own information. Most pharmaceutical companies have deep pockets and many streams of information. So when word got out, every pharmaceutical company in existence put together our itinerary and the gossip about a new drug and came up with Russell and me."

"So the news is out."

"So far it's just speculation. But that won't last long. The pieces aren't completely together yet but they will be soon and then someone will be on the next plane to the Amazon."

"They can track you to the Amazon but can they track you to where you went once you got there?"

"We used native transportation. Their canoes are the only ones that will get where we went. But if someone asks enough questions of enough people and throws enough money around, someone will remember us and where we went."

"Then it's a race to see who gets the drug first."

"I'm afraid so."

My father's face went rock-hard. "Then we'll just have to make sure we are first."

My mother hugged him. "I was hoping you'd say that." She took a deep breath. "It'll mean returning to the Amazon."

My father agreed. "But there'll be a lot to be done before we go traipsing all over the Amazon. Papers to file. Pharmaceutical companies to talk to because someone must manufacture this new drug. Contracts to be signed with the people who own the land where the drug is found." He began pacing again, faster and faster, thumping louder and harder. "Lots of things." He snapped his fingers. "So let's get started."

He stopped pacing long enough to look at Jace. "You'd better get going and bring Russell back ASAP so we can get a handle on this gargantuan project and do something. Start something."

Jace packed a small backpack, got the keys for the car at the end of the driveway, and asked me to drive him there on the four-wheeler so I could bring it back to the cabin in case we needed it while he was gone.

I started to climb behind him on the four-wheeler but he motioned for me to drive. "You'll have to drive back. Might as well get a feel for the driveway. And the mud." He got behind me and wrapped his arms around my waist as I started off as carefully and cautiously as I knew how.

His arms wrapped around me were pure carnal joy. His doubt about my ability wasn't. "This isn't the first time I've driven the driveway when it was muddy. It's a regular occurrence around here." But it was the first time I'd driven the four-wheeler with Jace wrapped around me as if I was a Christmas present. It was hard to breathe, hard to think and almost impossible to drive.

"I figured as much." His hands holding my middle were warm and solid. His voice was warm and not concerned that he was in danger from my driving. I noted that and wondered if he'd be so fearless if he knew how I was feeling. That I was so unnerved by his closeness that I'd be lucky to get us to the road alive. "When we get to the car I want to go over a couple of things with you."

"What things?"

"I'll tell you when we get there."

"You're waiting until we get there so I won't slide off the driveway in sheer terror because what you have to say will scare me to death?"

His breath was warm on my neck as he replied, "I don't wish to end up in a mud-filled ditch so, yes, that's pretty much the reason." He wasn't afraid but as I assessed what he'd said, I realized those arms around me were also near the controls. He was prepared to take over at a moment's notice should I screw up. Smart man.

CHAPTER 7

At the end of the driveway, he climbed off the four-wheeler so casually that I knew it wasn't casual at all. And he looked away as if looking at me would tell me something he wasn't read to say.

Good. At least I wasn't the only one affected by our closeness. "Remember to be safe. Not just you but also your parents. Because I won't be there if something goes wrong." He transferred his things from the four-wheeler to the car. "So I want you to concentrate on *how* to stay safe."

"Tell me how." I didn't have his background in danger and weapons and probably a lot more things I didn't know enough about to even begin to know my limitations. So, yes, I needed instructions.

"The most important thing is to stay close to the cabin. And I mean close. Do not even go to the edge of the forest. No wandering at all. No exploring. Stay within a few feet of the cabin."

I studied the muddy driveway. "It'll be useable shortly. If someone wants to get at us they'll be able to drive to the cabin. So even the cabin isn't safe."

"I hope to be back before that happens. I'll drive without stopping, sleep while this Russell guy packs, and drive straight back."

"What if the mud dries before you return?" Not likely but it could happen.

He paused before getting in the car. "Watch the driveway. If it dries up then stay on the deck so you'll see anyone coming. And take turns standing guard at night."

"And if someone does come?"

"Do you know how to shoot?"

"Gophers and snakes."

"People are no different. They make bigger targets so are easier to hit."

"I don't think I could shoot anyone."

"Of course not. Most people can't. But if you're holding the biggest, meanest-looking rifle your dad has in that gun safe and you point it at anyone coming to the cabin you won't have to shoot. They'll take one look at your weapon and leave as fast as possible."

I thought that over. "I hope so."

"I know so." Then he ruined everything by adding, "Unless he's a professional. Then, of course, nothing will stop him."

"What do I do then?"

"Pray. Then pull the trigger."

I decided to pray, instead, for more rain to keep the driveway impassable because that was more likely to keep us safe than anything I would actually do. I glanced at the cloudless sky and the oozing mud around us and knew it would take a lot of prayers.

Then I watched Jase accelerate down the gravel road in the first stage of his trip and returned to the cabin, examining the driveway for anything that would tell me when it would be dry enough for a vehicle to get through.

It rained that night. Not a downpour but enough rain that in the morning the driveway was once again a black, sticky morass. I silently cheered and thanked whomever had heard my prayers and hoped it would stay muddy forever.

My mother, on the other hand, frowned and loudly wished my father had included a decent driveway to the cabin when the place was remodeled. My father and I looked at each other as she pulled out frozen waffles and syrup and silently agreed that she hadn't yet internalized the seriousness of our situation. Of course not. Danger was normal for her and her globe-trotting partner. Why be concerned because of a little threat at home?

When breakfast was done I told my father what Jase had said and he went with me to the gun cabinet where we chose the largest, heaviest, ugliest rifle there, one that took six-inch shells and was capable of taking out even the most dangerous predators. Or really bad guys.

My father said, "I bought this thing when I was

with a bunch of guys who knew about guns and told me I should have it. Then I got it home and figured I'd been suckered because I'd never in my life have occasion to use a rifle like this one." He paused, then added wryly, "Guess they were right and I was wrong."

We loaded the rifle and leaned it against the wall beside the front door as my mother rolled her eyes skyward and did her best not to laugh at our over-the-top preparations for keeping us safe. But in her search for exotic drugs she'd traveled to all corners of the Earth and many had been dangerous. This was normal for her. Not for us.

I hung out on the deck all that day and the next watching for unwanted company but none came. The only arrival was Jase and Russell in my mother's car because by then the driveway was passable for an experienced driver who went so slowly that someone walking would get there first. That driver was Jase and there was no thought of him not making the trip safely.

He tried and failed to grab Russell's luggage when they got out of the car. The cantankerous, elderly explorer of unusual places had a fetish about other people handling his personal things so Jase was left to only carry his own back pack.

Our eyes met as he silently asked if there'd been any trouble and I replied with a slight shake of my head. He acknowledged my answer and went inside, noting the rifle beside the door without comment but with an approving nod and looking to see if anything else had changed. Nothing had and he took his things to his room. The room beside mine that I was sure held a gun somewhere. The cabin was beginning to resemble a fortress. Too bad the windows still made us vulnerable.

The next day was the promised day of talk and decisions. It was a lovely day so we adjourned to the deck to bask in sunshine, light breezes, and positive emotions. I wondered if we'd even notice any of those things once the meeting began.

"As I understand the situation, you two brilliant, educated, intrepid explorers have come upon something that can benefit mankind." My father's look bored into my mother and Russell. "Is that essentially correct?"

"Yes," they answered in concert.

Jace rose. "I'm not needed here. Mind if I take a walk?"

"You were hired for protection." It was a question. My father waited for an answer.

"I'd like to check out the layout of the land around here."

"Because attacks can come from anywhere, including the forest?"

Jace nodded that, yes, that was why. I rose to stand beside him. "I want to come with you."

Jace, my parents and Russell all shook their heads and vehemently said, "No!"

I stared them down. "I know the area. Jace doesn't. Whatever he hopes to accomplish will be done faster and better with me along." I folded my arms and continued to glare at them. "Besides, if Jace's job involves protection and I'm with him, doesn't that mean that if I go I'll be in the right place with the right person and, therefore, will be safe?"

They all wilted, even Jace, whose look my way said he'd get even with me for this obvious coercion when we were alone. I merely smiled a superior smile and went to get a light jacket as protection against insects and suggested that he, also, wear something over his short sleeved shirt or he'd regret it once we left the yard and entered the forest where the breeze wouldn't exist. When I returned, I carried insect repellant.

In the woods, he gladly applied the repellant when I'd finished dousing myself. "I didn't even think about mosquitoes."

"If the terrorists don't get you, the mosquitoes will."

He looked around, spotted a hill and headed towards it. "Can we get a feel for the area from there?"

"Our entire property and more. Lots more." In addition to the forest and the streams that meandered through it we'd be able to see several cabins though most blended in so well they'd not be noticed unless you knew where to look. Unless, of course, you were Jace Browne. I had no doubt he'd see everything down to the insects flitting from plant to plant. Had the military taught him how to see things no one else could? Or was it just another Jace thing?

He led the way up the hill and I followed, using the time to inspect Jace himself because it wasn't often I could stare at him without him knowing. I saw a physically top-of-the-line individual with a ground-eating stride that took into account the terrain we were traversing. He looked in every direction and saw everything and generally enjoyed the walk while still retaining the professional attitude that seemed to be part of his new job.

Dark hair, I knew his eyes were blue though I couldn't see them from behind, a face that was all planes and angles and totally male, a muscular, taller than average body and a general air of competence. In other words, he was one sexy dude and I enjoyed the view all the way to the top of the hill.

"Not many cabins in the area," was his first comment after giving the area a once-over. "Do you know who owns them and are they occupied?" In other words, might any of them contain bad guys?

I pointed to them one at a time, naming the families that owned them. "Plus there's one that's in limbo because the owner died and the family hasn't yet decided what to do about it." I pointed to a second cabin in the opposite direction. "And that one is owned by a company that lets its employees use it now and then. It's not large enough for company-wide meetings but they do use it for occasional smaller meetings and workshops, and I believe those employees who hunt and fish can stay there for free."

His look then followed the creeks that wound through the woods in no particular fashion until they disappeared elsewhere. "Too shallow for boats or even canoes," I said, answering his unasked question.

After we left the hilltop, we hiked through the forest for over a couple hours. I had no idea where we went or why but Jace seemed to know the layout of the forest from that brief glimpse from the top of the hill. It was slow going, climbing over fallen trees and struggling through patches of brush and across those creeks with our shoes and socks held high and the water biting cold on our bare feet.

We eventually circled back to that hill for one last look around. Then, as the sun started to dip towards the west we returned to the cabin, wondering if my parents and Russell had made any decisions while we were gone.

They had.

My father explained. "I'm going to finance this new drug, whatever it is. Find a pharmaceutical company to manufacture it and start the process to get it approved." He rubbed the back of his neck. "You'd think with a physician for a wife I'd know my way around the pharmaceutical world, but I don't so it's going to be a slow process."

Russell plonked his feet on the coffee table, completely at home in the cabin he'd visited many times. "I might know someone. Doesn't have any money, not since he made some bad business decisions a long time ago. Before Abigail and I met. Back then he financed my expeditions. When he went bankrupt, I thought I was out of the business of new pharmaceuticals until I met you, Gaylord."

"What's he doing now?"

"He's still in the pharmaceutical business but as a consultant instead of a financier. That's good for us because it means he not only knows the business he knows everyone in it and is current with everything that's happening. He should be able to match you with a company that's right for what we want to do. For a price, of course. He's money oriented."

Both my parents nodded assent. "Call him."

Russell said he'd have to do some digging for current contact information. "It shouldn't take long. With his help I'm confident we'll soon be in business."

My father began to pace, which, with his crutches was both interesting and painful to watch. "That'll take care of this end but there's still the origin of the drug. The tribe that knows about it and how to process it."

Russell added, "Without their special processing method it's just another green plant."

"We have to contact the tribe. Talk to them. Tell them what's going on and ask if they are interested in a deal. Then we'll see how they react."

"I hope they agree or the threats and danger we're in will have been for nothing."

My mother smiled. "I talked a bit with the tribal leaders before we left and I guarantee they are interested." Then she added, "Depending on the terms, of course."

We finished the day with steaks on the grill. My father did the honors, of course, while I made a salad and my mother watched without offering to help because she knew the best help she could give would be to stay out of our way.

I ended up next to Jace at the heavy wooden table on the deck. He was a healthy male with a healthy male's appetite. I didn't know why that made me feel good. He was just eating, for goodness sake. But it did.

As he looked around at all of us eating a normal meal, especially at Jace – definitely Jace and me beside him -- my father smiled that unreadable smile. Again. What was that smile about anyway and what about the meal on the deck had brought it out?

As we cleaned up afterwards, Jace caught my attention and we silently agreed that something was up with my father and that smile. Whatever he wanted with Jace was more than what he'd said so far. But neither of us had a clue what it was.

CHAPTER 8

The next day, Russell adjourned to the deck with his cell phone and proceeded to call his friend. Tried to call. Finally gave up in disgust because of our erratic cell service and retreated to the living room and the land line where he spent a few hours tracking his previous financier, Henry Torelle, while muttering things about expecting no cell service in the Amazon but it should exist in civilized society. He finally found Henry in a restaurant in New York.

Russell rolled his eyes when they were done talking. "He hasn't changed. The guy is lacking the brains of a flea." He sighed mightily. "But he knows everything and everyone you need for this particular project and he's a better negotiator than anyone else in the business." He sighed again. "And he's interested. He wants to talk." He looked at all of us. "But not here."

"Why not?" My father inspected what we still referred to as a cabin out of habit and not for any other reason. "Where can be better than here?" He didn't say 'safer' but that was what he meant.

"He insists on New York. Or any large, noisy, ugly city. He's a city person. He'd probably have a heart attack if he found himself surrounded by trees instead of skyscrapers."

Jace didn't like that idea. "What about security? Where can you meet where it's safe in New York? Do you know any places? And what about bodyguards? Do you plan to have them?"

"Surely that's overkill." Russell waved his hands aimlessly.

When he'd arrived he'd thought the whole bodyguard thing was a joke until he realized no one was laughing. He still thought we were overreacting. "I know about the threat to Brynn and being run off the road and, yes, Abigail and I had problems. But nothing came of them."

He went quiet for a long time. "I guess I tend to focus on those things that turn out alright and ignore what might happen next that might not end well." He shook his head as if trying to grasp what we were facing. But he didn't understand fear so he couldn't.

Jace had been thinking while everyone else talked. Now he spoke, bringing the conversation back to his specialty. Safety. "I have a fairly good mental picture of the surrounding forest. Thick trees and logging roads and creeks and thickets and so on. The thing is, people don't trek through thick brush and across creeks if there's an easier way to get where they are going. If anyone who wants to get here doesn't want to end up huffing and puffing and climbing over tree trunks and around swampy areas and getting twigs down their shirts, there are only a couple of paths they'll use and those can be staked out."

My father nodded. "What are you saying?"

"If you have trail cams, I can place them where there's the best chance of spotting someone who wants to come here via the back way. Through the woods." He finished with, "Everything that'll keep me informed who and what is in the area is a positive thing.

"We don't have any trail cams, but this is a rural area, lots of forest, so there's a sporting goods store in town that carries everything anyone could want for the outdoors. I'm sure they carry them." He nodded to Jace's car in the newly dry driveway. "Why don't you and Brynn head over there and see what you can find?" He handed Jace a credit card. "Get the best." He didn't have to add, 'because it might save lives.'

Jace didn't take the card. "I'd rather use cash."

My father paused and returned his credit card to his pocket. "Of course."

Jace explained. "If someone should trace the card, then they'd know there'll be trail cams around the cabin and they'll avoid the trails."

I shook my head. "I have a lot to learn."

Jace spoke low enough that only I could hear. "No reason to learn because this is temporary." Our eyes met but this time, unlike most times we'd communicated silently, I had no idea what he was thinking.

My father brought a wad of cash from his bedroom and handed it to Jace as he looked from Jace to me because, once again, he'd seen our silent communication. "Is this enough?"

Jace examined the bills and stuffed them in his pocket with a quiet smile. There were a lot of bills and they were all large denominations. "Should we also pick up a helicopter while we're shopping? I believe there's enough cash here for a decent one."

"If you know how to fly it."

He shook his head. "Propeller planes of all sizes and makes but not helicopters."

"Maybe a Beechcraft, then, instead of a helicopter."

"You don't have a runway."

"And there's not enough time to build one." My father inspected the nearby forest, clearly wondering if a runway and a small plane would fit our lifestyle. A slight shake of his head said it wouldn't. With a plane and a runway, the driveway wouldn't protect our solitude because someone could just fly in for a visit. Or to kidnap me.

Jace and I spent the better part of an hour in the nearby sporting goods store comparing trail cams. They had a number of them of all sizes and prices. Jace finally settled on the second most expensive. "The most expensive looks nice but doesn't do the job any better."

He asked the salesperson if they had a dozen in stock. They didn't but another store three towns over had what we wanted and would hold them for us if we went immediately.

Several hours later we had over a dozen trail cams in the back of Jace's SUV along with extra mosquito repellant and some netting that Jace wanted to help camouflage the cams. We headed back to the cabin with the satisfaction of an errand well done.

Jace had also picked up a Glock and a holster to hide it beneath a jacket. "I'm in the protection business now," he said by way of explanation. "I should be properly outfitted and a Glock is a decent weapon. Not large and not heavy but it'll get the job done." I tried not to let him see me shiver.

We returned to the cabin with the back of the SUV full of things I'd never have expected to deal with and soon we trudged into the forest on one of the four-wheelers pulling a garden cart full of cameras, a ladder, stuff to secure the cameras to trees with, and the camouflage netting to stick leaves and twigs into to do the same thing.

"I saw two trails when we were on the hill earlier," Jace said. "What can you tell me about them?"

We were on that hill we'd been on earlier looking one way and then another. I pointed. I couldn't see anything but forest but knew where the trail was that Jace had somehow picked out earlier. "That one follows a creek until it reaches a ridge. Then it follows the ridge. Between the creek and the ridge it meanders everywhere. Hunters like it because it eventually covers every square mile of the area. It was a game trail until people started using it. Now the animals avoid it."

"And the other trail?"

"It's a fairly direct route from the cabin I showed you earlier that belongs to the company I told you about. It connects that cabin to their property a few miles away."

"What's on the second property?"

"Nothing."

"Then why have it and why have a trail to it?"

"It was a good buy and now everyone who visits the cabin wants to take a walk through the forest to the additional property so they can boast about it later. The grounds-keeper made it an easy trail to follow. No one gets lost and they get lots of bragging rights about visiting nature and all that stuff."

"Which trail comes close to your cabin?"

"Both of them."

He sighed. "Of course they do. Where, exactly, do they come close?"

I pointed to two separate places and he inspected them carefully. "Okay. This is what we'll do. We'll put trail cams where the trails come close to the cabin. Two cams on each trail just before they reach the closest place to the cabin so we'll see anyone coming from either direction. Then we'll distribute the rest of the cams along the trails and at select spots off the trails in places where people who know how to travel off trails might go."

"It's pretty thick."

"There are always clear areas. Do you know where they are?"

I nodded. "My family has had the cabin for generations. I've been coming here all my life. I know these woods like the back of my hand."

"Good. Then when the cameras are installed no one should be able to sneak up on you or your family."

As an afterthought, he pointed to an additional cabin "What about that one?"

I waved my hand to the surrounding forest. "There are cabins that you can't see for the trees. Small cabins, usually for summer use only. Some have roads to them. Some can only be reached by hiking."

He sighed and raked a hand through his hair. "This gets worse and worse."

"But those other cabins are mostly empty, only occupied when the owners are there for vacations. The company cabin is the only one that's usually occupied, either by company personnel or people who rent it for a few days."

He squinted at the miles of green forest spread out below us. "If the company cabin is available for rent then it's the most likely, so we'll concentrate on it."

His eyes crinkled as he considered the best options. Sunlight filtered through the trees, turning him into a dappled statue. Maybe a statue of a Greek god. I thought again, as I'd thought many times since he'd come into my life, that he was a fantastic example of the male of the species. Which was good for securing cameras to high places in trees. Which was the only reason I was thinking such thoughts. No other reason at all.

At least I tried to convince myself that was the only reason I was covertly watching him. His physical prowess. I lied to myself, of course, and knew I was lying. But, I reasoned, he'd never know how he affected me because he'd be gone soon enough unless he went to work for my father permanently as he was thinking of doing. But if he left, then eventually I'd forget what he looked like soon after.

I didn't know how many hours we spent leaning the ladder against tree trunks, then going from them to sturdy branches that we straddled while fastening the cameras so they pointed at the trail. Then we either pulled branches close to them to disguise them or arranged netting around them for the same purpose.

When we were about half way done, with an expression of pained irritation, Jace blew away pine needles that threatened to blind him. I took a look at him and laughed. He tried to look insulted and failed and ended up laughing along with me while wriggling in an attempt to shake loose all those itchy needles that had gotten into his shirt. "Laugh if you will and I itch like crazy, but these trail cams will give you peace of mind even if they prove unnecessary."

He blew away most of the remaining pine needles and joined me on the ground, folding the ladder and laying it on the trailer behind the four-wheeler as I prepared to head for the next stop, a huge oak tree that would give us a perfect view of anyone coming along that same trail from the opposite direction. There was a kind of order to the trail cam locations. The forest wasn't uniform and people would choose the easy ways through over others that were more difficult. Jace knew which ways they'd go even better than me, the native who grew up there.

When we were finished, he inspected our work before we climbed back on the four-wheeler. He gave a satisfied nod. "We'll soon know exactly what's in the forest."

I liked the idea for more than safety sake. "Not just bad guys. If we're lucky, we'll see babies. Fawns or kits or maybe young bears learning to hunt."

"They'll never know they are being spied upon. Bad guys won't know either."

I shook myself and danced about so the twigs and leaves that had found their way into my clothes and were itching me to death would fall out before we returned home. Most of them, anyway. I'd take a shower as soon as possible and was pretty sure Jace would do the same though after being laughed at I figured he'd possibly decide to be the stoic male and pretend the twigs I saw sticking out of his shirtsleeves didn't bother him. But he couldn't fool me. He was itching just as badly as I was.

Sure enough, when we reached the cabin he headed straight to his room with its attached bathroom, even before reporting to my father who was eager to learn how to watch the cameras by using the computer sitting on a desk in an alcove off the main room. The computer he'd said he'd never use because the cabin was for rest and solitude and not for connecting with the larger world. The one that was actually used constantly by everyone.

When Jace joined the family in the main room, he smelled like soap and was wearing clean clothes. As was I. Our glances to one another said how much we appreciated the niceties of civilized life. Like hot showers. My father intercepted that look and smiled. Again. The man always intercepted looks between Jace and me and he always smiled. This time he smiled a second time and bestowed a beneficent look on us. As usual every time Jace and I connected in any way.

Whatever was behind that smile as he looked from Jace to me and back again even before asking about the trail cams? It was almost as if Jace and I were first in his thoughts whenever he saw us communicate silently and staying alive somehow become second. I wished I knew what he was thinking every time he smiled that smile.

Sometimes being my father's daughter could be very frustrating.

CHAPTER 9

While Jace and I were installing the trail cams and getting twigs and pine needles down our backs and in our clothes, Russell Manners had been busy. My parents and Russell explained as we all settled around that huge wooden picnic table that looked rustic and had cost as much as a small car. My mother had practically had a heart attack at my father's choice of table but later admitted it was nice that it wouldn't blow over in even the most severe windstorm as was also true of the heavy log-type chairs that came with it.

"We're heading for New York," my father explained to catch us up on their plans. "All of us." He cast a significant look at Jace. "You to protect Brynn, of course, while her mother, Russell, and I meet with this Henry Torelle."

Jace's frown said he didn't like that plan. "I was hoping to watch the tail cams for a few days to get a sense of what's normal in the forest."

My father frowned also. "So you'll recognize aberrant traffic when it happens?" His shoulders slumped with this unexpected thought. "Understandable and important but in the city we'd be together in one place which is good for being safe."

Jace folded his arms across his chest. "Where will you be staying?" His unspoken question was whether it would be as safe as the forest.

"Our apartment. Brynn has her own apartment, of course, but she should stay with us for now because our building is secure."

Jace gave a quick nod. "If the apartment is safe, then you don't need me there."

My father frowned a second time, deeper this time. He bit his bottom lip, shook his head a couple times, blinked the way he did when he was thinking hard, and said, "If you won't be there, then I don't want Brynn there either."

"Why not?" Jace's eyebrows rose. "You said it's safe."

My father thought fast. I could see it in the way his eyes moved back and forth. I'd known him all my life so I knew he was about to come up with something on the spur of the moment to make sure Jace and I remained together even if that meant he remained at the cabin and I stayed there too. But he came up with a good enough reason. I gave him credit for quick thinking. "If Brynn goes with us and you aren't there, then she'll have to stay in our apartment. She'll be a prisoner. Because she can't wander about the city alone and we'll be busy."

He scowled as he came up with additional arguments. They were valid but not important, merely additional reasons for me sticking close to Jace. My father definitely believed he'd keep me safe and was making sure he was close enough to me to do so while pretending there were other reasons. "She hates the city, always did, and she loves it here. She's always complaining there's nothing to do in New York. Nothing worth doing anyway."

He finished triumphantly with, "So she'll be better off here than in New York if you aren't there. If you come, then she can enjoy what the city has to offer as long as you are with her. Either way works as long as you stick close to her."

His face broke into one of those unreadable and totally complacent smiles I'd known all my life. "You seem to know what you're doing so if you truly want to check out the trail cams, she can stay too." He dared Jace to argue. Jace didn't and since I preferred the forest to the city, Jace and I stayed behind.

The three of them didn't leave immediately. They called to make sure the apartment hadn't been broken into, something no one had thought to do until Jace suggested it. My mother's eyes went wide, a movement that said how hard the possibility hit her. But she'd not yet internalized the seriousness of the danger we were in. Russell just shrugged. As usual. The man was implacable.

My father's eyebrows rose in satisfaction once again, convinced he'd made the right choice of Jace for security because obviously Jace's thought process was way better than ours where security was concerned. Like how to think about apartments even if you weren't there.

"I'd like to speak with you in private before we leave," he said to Jace when we'd all once more absorbed the concept that we were in danger and must think ahead to each and every situation. My father nodded to Jace with the expression I was familiar with that said what was to come was important. Hugely important. "I'd like to go over a few things." Then he added diffidently, "If you're not busy."

"Okay." Jace agreed with equal diffidence, matching my father's expression. I was pretty sure Jace also read my father's expression, but was pretending otherwise. Or else he truly didn't know whether my father's expression meant anything or not.

I caught Jace's attention and gave a slight tip of my head to indicate that we should meet privately before he had that talk with my father. Because I knew that when my father pretended indifference, whatever was on his mind was of great importance. Jace's half blink said he'd got the message.

As soon as it seemed a normal thing to do, I said I was thirsty after our forest adventures. I headed for the kitchen and a drink. Jace said he, too, would like something, and followed me.

We grabbed pop from the refrigerator, and I led him out the kitchen door to the deck and then beyond, around the cabin to the back where there was no possibility of anyone following and hearing what I was about to say.

Jace looked a question to me.

I began. "I could be over reacting."

Jace laughed. "If it's about your father – and I suspect it is because your expression changed the moment he suggested the two of us have a little talk – then you can't possibly be over reacting."

"He can be a bit over the top."

"Which is why you are going to warn me about him. Before he and I have our little talk. So I'll be prepared for whatever he comes up with."

I laughed and wondered how Jace had managed to cut through to the essence of things, though when I thought back to the time since we'd met I realized he seldom spoke much or for long but what he said always made sense.

"So what exact quirk of your father's are you warning me about now?" He chugged his pop and waited for my answer as the sun glinted off the can and onto him and turned him into some kind of heavenly being. Except there was nothing angelic about him. He was totally human, absolutely male, and more competent than most. Of that I had no doubt. "And why do you think I should be on guard when we have that talk?"

"I know my father so I'm sure your little chat will be where he tells you what he's been thinking about all along. What he wants from you. What he's been planning ever since you saved his life and decided you are perfect for – something." I paused for a few seconds. "I just don't know what that something is and want you to be prepared for anything."

"Because you believe it might send me into shock?"

"It's happened to other people who've had little talks with him."

He grinned. "I'm not a kid. I've been around. I consider myself to be shock proof."

I examined him. He was solid, with his feet planted firmly apart and his entire body looking like a weapon if anyone tried anything. "I agree that you appear shock proof." I couldn't disagree with his assessment of himself. The man was the epitome of common sense. "But my father is my father."

"So you expect the meeting will be an irresistible force meeting an immovable object?"

"Very possibly."

He grinned even more. A sudden, wide smile of complete self-confidence. "Don't worry. And I'll let you know how it turns out. If you are interested."

"Please do. I can't imagine what's been on his mind all this time. Usually I can figure it out but this time I don't have a clue."

"It'll probably be about pay and that kind of thing. Nothing special."

"Maybe." But I doubted it would be so simple. I knew my father. And I didn't trust him, not when he wore that expression.

Our pop finished, we returned to the cabin, tossed our empty cans in the recycle bin and returned to the main room where my father, Russell, and my mother were finishing their plans for leaving the next morning.

My mother would drive, my father would be in the front seat with his crutches and Russell would nap in the back seat because years of travel through some of the most primitive regions of the planet in his quest for new pharmaceuticals had taught him to sleep whenever and wherever he could. And because he was elderly and needed more sleep than most.

Jace turned to my father. "Do you want to learn how the trail cam system works?"

Of course he did and so did the rest of us. So we adjourned to the room containing computers that had been set aside for guests to get some work done which happened oftener than I'd expected. My father's friends tended to be as driven as he was and meltdown was a concern if they strayed too far from computers or were away from the internet for more than an hour or two.

My father had his own office in a corner room with sunlight coming from two angles and it contained the computer he swore he never used. Of course he lied and he loved that office. I wouldn't have been surprised if he moved to the cabin permanently just to use the office and watch the deer beyond those mullioned windows while he worked.

It took Jace a while to connect the computers in the guest office to the cameras we'd installed in trees. My father offered to help and soon the two men had a guy-technology-internet thing going and forgot I existed.

I watched and didn't say what I was thinking, that they resembled little kids with new playthings. Then I remembered why the cameras were in all those trees and why we needed to monitor them twenty-four seven and the urge to laugh died before I made a sound.

Eventually we could see what the cameras saw, switching from one to another at will or we could set them to switch automatically every minute or so. When it was on automatic we could see everything coming or going along both paths through the forest in a short span of time.

The first thing we saw when the system was up and running was a smallish bear poking its face into one of the cameras. My father pointed to it. "I'll bet that's the nuisance bear that's been trying to get in our garbage. Wakes me up at night banging on the cans. I had to bring them into the garage." And a family of racoons out for a walk. A couple of German Shepherd dogs doing nothing in particular. Or wolves. They didn't wear collars and I couldn't tell the difference. I decided they were wolves because that was more romantic.

Jace watched the dogs. Or wolves. Whatever they were. "I wonder what they do when people come along the trails." The dog/wolves looked around, then slowly sauntered out of camera range. "And how hunters react if they come across a pair of wolves when they are hiking."

My father saw the wolf/dog episode differently. "Do you think I should invest in a guard dog or two?"

Jace shook his head. "It would be good if you already had one but to get one now would be a waste of time because by the time you got it trained the problem will be resolved."

"I suppose we don't need guard dogs," my father said as he watched the empty forest where moments earlier there had been a pair of wolves. Or dogs. "As long as we have the trail cams and you are here to keep things going smoothly and safely."

He looked at Jace. "Speaking of which, if you have time I'd like to have that little talk with you now."

Jace nodded and followed my father into his office. I looked around for something to do while they talked, thinking how quickly I'd gotten used to having Jace around. It had only been a few days and already I didn't know what to do with myself without him.

I loved solitude, I should have a thousand things I wanted to do but I couldn't think of a single one as I stared at the closed door to my father's office and wondered how long the 'little talk' would take and what they'd be talking about. Or, rather, what my father would talk about while Jace listened.

Two cans of pop and a slice of chocolate cake later, the door opened and Jace walked out. I took one look at his face and almost choked on the cake. There was only one word to describe his expression. He was stunned.

The man who considered himself to be shock proof was walking without knowing what he was doing or where he was going. He didn't even see me as I got over the choking fit that anyone could hear a mile away. I finished my cake and went to him.

I leaned close so he'd become aware I existed because at the moment he didn't. "What did he say? What did he do? What on earth could possibly make you look like you look now?"

My voice brought him back to reality. He turned to me and just stared for a long time without saying a word. Then he shook his head in an effort to regain control of himself because he'd clearly been told something so unexpected that he didn't know how to handle the news. What to do with himself. How to react.

He was mere feet from me because I'd gone close to him. Now he backed up a bit. Looked at me and turned beet red. Licked his lips and tried to speak. Finally he got control of his voice and cleared his throat. "We need to talk. You and me."

"Now?"

He looked back at my father's office. The door was still open but my father had remained inside. Jace stared through that open door and shook his head. "No. Not now. Now while he's still here. But soon. After they leave. Not before."

"That'll be morning. Twelve hours at least. Can't you tell me now?"

He shook his head. "Not now. Not yet."

"Why not?"

"Because I can't." He looked harried. Jace never

looked harried. "It was unexpected. And -- unusual." He moved close and took my hands in his. Stared at me, truly seeing me for the first time since leaving my father's office. "I promise to tell you everything in the morning."

At that moment my father emerged from his office. He glanced our way and saw our joined hands. He smiled and looked like he'd just been given a Christmas present. Or two. Or three. Then without a word he went to find my mother and help her pack for their trip.

CHAPTER 10

The next morning, the trio left as the sun rose. Since it was summer, that was quite early but they had hours of driving ahead of them.

"I should be with them," Jace said.

"Out of an abundance of concern for their safety?"

"Yep." He raked a hand through his hair. "But I can't be in two places at once and this is where your father wants me to be." His tousled hair blew every which way in the early morning breeze that changed the air from night to day as the early birds started talking to each other and the night animals disappeared. "So this is where I stay."

I liked his hair riffling in the breeze. He wasn't a neat freak but always seemed so put together that any part of him that dared to not be as it should got my attention. Which made me wonder. What would it be like to run my fingers through that mane of hair?

With a start I realized what I was thinking and pulled my mind back to the matters at hand. Like what he and my father had talked about the day before that had gotten the unflappable man in front of me so shook up that he needed an entire night to think about it before letting me in on what had transpired.

I stepped in front of him, stopping him, daring him to ignore me. "Okay, Jace. It's morning. You've had a night to think and you promised you'd tell me everything." I folded my arms, spread my legs apart, and stared him down.

He relented. Took a step backwards. Looked to the right and then to the left, but there was nothing in either direction to help him out of what he obviously considered a difficult situation. He raked his hand through his hair again, making that tousled head of hair even more messy.

Then he looked at me, trying to give himself more time before having to come clean with what had been said. Then he sighed mightily and suggested we make some breakfast and bring it out on the deck. "Then I'll tell you everything."

"Everything? Every single little tidbit? Promise?"

He nodded with an expression much like that of a condemned man on the way to the gallows. "I promise." But he needed the extra time provided by cooking and carrying things outside to figure out how to tell me what had happened.

Why? What could my father possibly have said to affect him so?

When we were finally settled and chugging coffee and inspecting the sausage and scrambled eggs on our plates, I glared at him over the rim of my cup, daring him to find still another excuse to delay speaking. "So what did you and my father discuss?" I smiled sweetly, set my cup down, and glared some more. And waited.

He sighed deeply. Raked a hand through his hair. Again. Wiggled uncomfortably. "It's not so much what we discussed because there was no discussion."

"What you are saying is that there was just my father talking and you listening." As per usual with my father.

"Yep."

"So what did he say that has the unflappable Jace Browne all shook up?"

"The first topic was that you need a bodyguard."

I nodded. "No surprise there."

I nodded again encouragingly because that information was obviously not important but we had to get past it before getting to the part that had him tied up in knots. Jace said, "And he wants me to take the job."

"Which you had already agreed to." The day after my father's accident and again, later. "And I'm assuming the pay is adequate." He nodded, which didn't surprise me because I knew my father. Generous to a fault. So I simply waited and watched for what would come next.

"Ummm.." He spoke so cautiously that I knew we were finally getting to the important stuff. "How much do you know about security, Brynn? Protection? Bodyguards and such?"

The question set me thinking. "Not much."

"I've never worked in security before but I know guys who have. It's something former military types often go into after leaving the military." A bluebird flew above us. He followed its flight until it disappeared, giving him a bit of a delay. "There are rules that go with the job. I know the rules."

"What are the rules?"

"How to keep people safe is the big one. But the next biggest – sometimes the most important rule – is no fraternization with the client."

"What's wrong with being friendly?"

"Friendly is okay as long as the security professional doesn't get *too* friendly."

I nodded. "Because it can make the guard less alert?"

"That's part of it. But in general it's just not a good idea to get too close to someone you are protecting. Or with your coworker if you're talking about people working regular jobs instead of protection. Most jobs have rules that say kind of that same thing."

"Because too much fraternization can lead to problems later."

"Exactly."

"And my father warned you against fraternizing with me?" I huffed a bit and gulped my coffee down hot and fast as anger began somewhere deep in me. "Because if that's what you're having so much trouble telling me, then next time I see my father I'll give him a piece of my mind because that's ridiculous."

How dare my father be so controlling! I warmed up to my subject as my anger increased. "You and I didn't meet in the usual way professional security types meet their clients. You helped my father when he was injured and warning you away after that and after we became friends isn't going to happen!" The more I thought about it the angrier I got.

He put up a hand to stop me. "He didn't do that. He never said anything about us not being friends."

My mouth dropped open. "Then what did he say?"

"He *wants* us to be friendly. And that's the problem."

"Why is it a problem?"

He wiggled. Flushed a bit. Looked for that bluebird but it was long gone. And sighed again. "Not just friends. He made it very clear that he hopes we will become more than friends."

"What?!" If my mouth wasn't already open, it would have dropped a mile. "He wants *what*?"

"He wants me to push it. To do what I can to develop a relationship with you."

"What kind of relationship?" His face turned redder. "Are you saying he suggested a *romantic* relationship?"

"Yep." He managed to not look away but it was hard.

"That's insane!"

"He said if we become more than friends it'll be fine with him. If we develop a romantic relationship that'll be even better. If we should happen to fall in love and get married, I got the impression he'll be in seventh heaven."

I managed to close my mouth and thought hard to the extent I was able to think at all after such an announcement. Finally I managed to speak in a squeaky voice. "Are you saying that my father is on the lookout for a son-in-law?"

"It seems that way."

"And he's chosen you?"

"It appears so."

"Oh my goodness."

The inane words were all I could think to say. But as I examined the man across the table from me, I realized he was exactly the kind of man my father would choose to become part of the family. Rough. Tough. Competent. Intelligent. Independent. And so on.

But coming right out and suggesting it?! I was blown away.

Jace leaned back and ignored his breakfast much the same as I was ignoring mine. Except for the coffee. He gulped down a cup and went for more. When he returned he dropped back into his chair and looked me in the eye for the first time that morning. "It's because he's worried about your future. He said the vultures are beginning to circle."

"Vultures?"

"Potential husbands. He called them vultures."

I laughed. Couldn't help it, remembering the men I'd introduced to my father, the ones I'd taken a leave of absence and come to the cabin to avoid. "As to that, he's somewhat right. If you could see the guys I've met lately, you'd shudder."

"That bad?"

"They're either rich and believe we'll make a good pair because we are both rich or they don't have any money but think they can charm me into marrying them so they can become rich. Two kinds of guys and both kinds are obsessed with money. And there don't seem to be any other kinds of guys around, at least not that I've met."

"Sounds awful."

"It is, but I ignore them."

"You father is afraid one of them might get you to fall in love with him."

I snorted. "He should know me better than that."

"He's protective of his little girl. You can't blame him for that."

"I can blame him for trying to run my life."

"Not run it. Just give nature a helping hand."

"That's what he said?"

"His exact words."

I leaned back and looked for that bluebird myself because I needed a distraction from the direction this conversation was going. I willed it to appear. But the sky remained empty of everything except the sun that had finally decided to stick around and keep the driveway dry plus an occasional cloud drifting aimlessly in the summer blue sky.

Time passed. The awkwardness between us grew. I had to say something because the silence was stretching so thin it was about to snap. "So what do we do now?"

I ignored the sky in favor of concentrating on the man across the table even though I felt my face flush as our glances met. I forced myself to lean a bit closer, too, to prove to myself that I could still do so without imploding.

He, also, leaned across the table towards me until we were so close I could feel his breath. "That's what you need to decide, Brynn. What you want to do about it. What you want me to do about it." Steam from our coffee rose between us, making everything slightly unreal. "Because you're his daughter and the one most affected."

"If he gets what he wants, you'll be affected too." I didn't touch on how I'd be affected. No reason for him to know how wonderful that would be. Not in a million years would I admit it.

He got up and got still more coffee. When he returned he gulped it and almost spit it out because it was so hot it burned his mouth. Then he said, "Yes, it'll affect me too. Of course it will." If anything, his face turned even redder. "But you're his main concern."

I softened. "I can understand his position. Part of why he's so successful is that he cares about people. Including his family. But another part of that success is because he truly believes he knows what's best for each and every person in his world and he works hard to make whatever that is happen."

"Including to you"

"He's been trying to run my life since I was a kid. For my own good, of course. I've learned to ignore him." I looked into Jace's eyes. Straight into them, as deep as I could see, and those eyes were fathomless. "And now Jace Browne, he thinks he knows what's best for you too."

"And he thinks what's best for me is you." Not a question. A statement.

"Evidently. And vice versa. Me and you together no matter which direction you look at us from."

We were silent for a while. Then Jace spoke. "I was ambivalent about my future when I saw someone run him off the road. I was looking for a place to settle down." The words were said warily. Slowly. As a diversion? Or possibly because, in Jace's mind, they pertained to our current situation?

"Have you found that place?" My question was stilted because I had no idea where this was going. In fact I had the sensation of skating on thin ice. My father had finally gone too far and this whole idea was foolish in the extreme. Wasn't it?

Jace looked around before continuing. His gaze took in the forest, the hills, the general layout of the place I'd known all my life. Finally he spoke. "This is a nice place. I like the forest. The privacy. Everything about it. So, yes, maybe I've found what I was looking for. Here. The forest, I mean." Then he looked directly at me. Through me. All of me. He blinked slowly. Looked at me again. Moved because he couldn't stay still any longer. And repeated, "Because it's nice. All of it. Very nice."

His blush had faded but now it returned full force and my face was just as red. I didn't have the courage to ask him to be more specific but just wondering what he meant by 'nice' sent a buzzing sensation through me that was entirely due to the man across the table inspecting every inch of me in a different way than before he and my father had a talk. Neither could I look at him the same way I'd done until then. And of course the buzzing went straight to the core of my very being. I felt things I'd never felt before and was stupefied by how strong those feelings were.

I wished I knew what he'd meant by his last remark. Did he include me in the things he regarded as nice? Maybe? Possibly? Just a little bit?

He finally spoke. "So maybe I'll stick around. For a while, at least." Then he went silent. "Because it's nice here. And to see how things work out. The job and so forth." And I knew the conversation was over.

We gave up on breakfast. The food was cold by then, anyway, and sausage and eggs couldn't compete with life-altering possibilities. Or with my father. We carried the uneaten food across the yard and dumped it at the edge of the forest and hoped it would be eaten by squirrels instead of bears that might come back for seconds.

We put our dishes in the dishwasher and refilled our cups with more hot, strong coffee and stood in the middle of the kitchen and stared at one another because neither of us had the slightest idea how to get past my father's preposterous proposition.

CHAPTER 11

As we stood in awkward silence, we heard a ping. Jace went on alert. "Something is on one of the trails. The computer pings when anything moves."

We investigated. The computer screen showed a man walking along a forest trail. I checked the printout that told which camera we were watching, so I knew it was on the trail from the cabin owned by the largish company that let employees use it for hunting and fishing and general vacationing. "Probably nothing. Just some corporate type out for a stroll."

"I want to watch for a while." Our embarrassing conversation was forgotten, shoved aside as we concentrated on a stranger walking through the nearby forest.

The walker went out of camera range and disappeared until he reached the next trail cam. Then the walker reappeared as he slowed and stopped in perfect camera range and looked around. I hoped we'd camouflaged the camera well enough for it to remain hidden. Though his look flicked over the branch where the camera was hidden, his gaze kept moving without hesitating, and I breathed a sigh of relief. Beside me, Jace did too and muttered low. "We did good, Brynn."

Then Jace did something else. He reached out and took my hand, seemingly unaware of what he was doing, and we stood that way as we watched the walker take a drink from a water bottle and replace it in a carrier around his waist. Then he turned, examining his surroundings a bit more closely, and stepped off the trail.

"He's not looking at the camera so that's not what caught his attention. He's looking at something beyond camera range." Jace's hand gripped mine harder. I wondered if he realized how hard he was holding my hand as his concentration on the screen became complete. "What does he see?" Would he hold my hand if he realized he was doing so?

"Nothing dangerous. No bears or cougars or he wouldn't be walking towards it. He'd be going away."

"I wish we could see what he sees."

"Do you think it's important?"

"Let's find out."

"How?"

"The cameras can be rotated. He's going away from it so he won't notice the movement. So I think it's safe to move it and see what he's looking at." Jace moved a joystick and the scenery changed. "That should do it."

We went closer to the screen to better see what the walker had spotted, Jace pulling me along, still seemingly unaware of his action. It was like looking over the man's shoulder as he moved away from the camera and towards a slight parting in the trees that created a long sight line in what would normally be thick forest.

As soon as he got past the thick trees, he stopped,

folded his arms, and examined the view along the narrow corridor between trees. He took out a pair of binoculars and looked through them to see better. As we saw what he was looking at, my breath stopped.

"It's our cabin."

"He's watching us."

Visions of the police went through my mind. I thought back to where I'd left my twenty-two. And where were Jace's guns? I glanced at him. The bulge at his waist from his Glock made me feel better. "Should I call the police?"

He squeezed my hand that he still held. So, yes, he knew what he was doing. "He's most likely just out for a stroll and happened to notice the cabin because of the opening in the trees and is wondering who the neighbors are."

"Is that what you truly believe?"

He shrugged. Pulled me close and wrapped his arms around me much the way a parent might comfort a frightened child and I was glad to have the Jace from before that conversation with my father back. The one who did more than hold hands. The one whose mere presence made me feel safe because the longer the situation we were in continued the more I needed that Jace. Maybe he wouldn't stick around. Maybe I'd see the new Jace as soon as the man watching us disappeared. But for now I felt right. "I have no idea what he's thinking but I don't intend to panic just because he's looking over this cabin. It's a large building. An architect's dream. A beautiful log house in the forest. And it's noticeable."

"So I should stop panicking?" No sense pretending I wasn't panicking because it was obvious. "I should laugh about it?" I leaned harder into Jace's body and paid more attention to how that felt than to what I saw on the camera.

"I've set the cameras to record everything so we have a good picture of him if something later on makes us think he's doing more than just looking." Jace's voice said the man could be anything from a casual hiker to a dirtbag out to do us harm.

Just then the man put the binoculars away and pulled out a camera from a backpack. He snapped several pictures of the cabin. Jace's arms around me tightened and his voice, when he spoke, was guarded. "It could still just be a hiker taking a picture of a dream cabin in the forest." He rested his chin on my hair. "Your cabin is perfect for that. Very picturesque. But tonight I will sleep in front of your bedroom door. Just in case."

He already slept as close to me as possible without being over zealous and he did so every night so, though his words were to make me feel better, as far as I was concerned he couldn't be any closer than he was. Unless he was in my bedroom. If so, I decided, I'd like that. It would be the ultimate safe feeling.

So thinking, I moved in his arms, turning to look at him. "Not in front of the door. In the room with me. We have folding beds and mattresses so you can be comfortable." I added, "With a folding bed you won't have to sleep on the floor."

"The floor, huh?" I felt his breath on my hair as he chuckled. "You aren't objecting to me spending the night in your bedroom? Especially after my talk with your father?"

"He didn't suggest you sleep in my room. I did." I

laughed along with Jase as the hiker returned to the path and continued on his way, eventually leaving camera range so the screen went black. "I'm inviting you to sleep in my bedroom and I'm not even blushing."

His reply was droll. "Just so you understand. Your father would approve."

I laughed again and was almost grateful to that stranger on the forest path who'd got us past my father's ridiculous proposal and he'd done so in a way that we could laugh about it. "My father will never know."

"I hope not. When he returns, we'll tell him about the hiker but not the enhanced overnight security precautions."

Jace probably thought it would work that way. But I knew my father. He'd know the truth. I'd never know how he'd figure it out except that it would be the same way he'd figured out every single secret I'd had as a child. So of course he'd know this one, too.

But I had no plan to tell Jace to sleep elsewhere because with him near my bed with a Glock beneath his pillow, I'd sleep too. Like a babe. Safe. Cared for.

I privately acknowledged that Jace and I were superficially heading for exactly what my father wanted. We weren't really, of course. It was a security thing, nothing romantic about it. But I couldn't help but wonder if the fates had arranged for that hiker to do the precise thing that would put Jace on high alert and send me into panic mode and into his arms and thus create what could be a suggestive situation.

My life was interesting and getting more so every day. "I've decided how to handle my father's wishes," I said as a way to take my mind off the coming night. I explained, "In case you are interested."

"Definitely interested. What do you suggest we do?"

"We ignore what he said. We live our lives as if he'd never said a word."

"Sounds good to me." But his arms were still around me and that made his words irrelevant even as he didn't seem to be aware of us so close together even though I knew he was. I, on the other hand, was so sensitive to him next to me that I felt like I'd stuck my finger in an electric socket, only in a good way. I just wished he gave some indication of feeling the same. But he didn't. I couldn't read him at all.

I was surprised that it wasn't awkward when I showed Jace where the spare bedding was kept, along with the folding beds that he ignored because a mattress on the floor would be fine. Nor did it bother either of us as we got ready for the night in our respective bathrooms.

Even as we climbed into bed, me in a real bed, Jace on that mattress on the floor, and talked about nothing in particular and everything in general there was no awkwardness. Just a continuation of what we did during the day.

We were getting past my father's ridiculous suggestion. I wasn't sure if that was bad or good.

I pulled my blankets high, rolled onto my side, closed my eyes, and expected to fall asleep instantly. I did sleep that night, though not immediately. Instead I found myself listening to the breathing of the man nearby and the listening went on for hours. I was sure I was still wide awake far after midnight.

I knew each time he rolled from one side to the

other. I tensed twice when something got his attention and his hand slowly slid beneath his pillow where he kept the Glock. I relaxed each time that hand left the pillow empty because whatever he'd heard hadn't been a problem. And, eventually, I slept. Late, but better than never.

I slept until sometimes in the depths of the night. It was still pitch black. Close to morning but not close enough for the faint graying of the sky that meant day would follow.

A sound woke me.

I came instantly awake and knew Jace had done the same. He didn't say anything. He didn't have to, he knew I was awake and alert. I felt more than heard his hand slide beneath the pillow once more and this time when it came out it was holding the Glock.

The sound came again. It was at the window. As silently as a panther, Jace somehow got up from his mattress on the floor in one smooth movement and onto my bed. Then he was lying on the bed beside me and half on top of me, keeping me still with one arm and holding the Glock with the other. He pointed it at the window as another soft sound came. It was just a whisper. But it was a whisper that didn't belong.

Slowly, silently, as we watched the rectangle that was the huge window that shone with the slightly lighter black than inside the room, we saw the screen being removed and set aside. Then the window opened a crack but no one could be seen opening it, not for a while. Whoever it was waited patiently to see if he'd raised an alarm.

When he knew no alarm had been triggered, an arm pushed the window open as high as possible. It was a large window, all the new windows from the remodel were large to let in as much light as possible. They could also easily admit a person.

Jace raised the Glock. Aimed. But at the precise moment he squeezed the trigger, a sound beyond the cabin, a night owl, startled whomever was breaking in and they jumped so the bullet went wide. Then we heard running feet pounding the deck along with low swearing as whoever was out there ran away.

Then we heard nothing. Jace flew from the bed in one swift motion. "Don't turn on the light," he yelled as he ran through the cabin to the front door in the direction of the running feet. "In case there's a second intruder. Keep your twenty-two ready." I grabbed the rifle from where it leaned against the wall beside the head of my bed and held it tight.

Then I dropped to the side of the bed away from the window and stayed there because I didn't know what else to do, clutching the twenty two as I moved. And I waited for something to happen.

I heard Jace reach the deck. I heard his swearing, long and angry. I'd not heard him swear before. When he'd vented his anger, he returned to the bedroom and switched on the light. "He's gone."

"Was there just one?"

"I only saw one. I doubt there was time for anyone else to get away without being seen or heard and my shot would have sent anyone nearby running for their life." He looked around the room, into the corners, daring anyone else to show themselves. "It was most likely the man from this afternoon."

"And we have his picture."

"We do indeed." He checked the time. "And I'll

stay up till dawn. Just in case."

"Me too."

"You can sleep. I'll keep watch."

I disagreed. "There's no way I can sleep after what happened." He nodded reluctant agreement and didn't argue as I asked, "How about coffee?" Our usual response to whatever happened. We'd drunk a lot of coffee lately.

He nodded that coffee would be good and I headed to the kitchen and used the shiny cappuccino machine no one else could figure out how to use to make something special to take my mind off the fact that my home had just been invaded and I'd been attacked. When it was ready, we sat across from one another with the Glock and the twenty-two on the table between us and waited for dawn.

"If I'd been alone, he'd have succeeded."

"I sleep in your room from now on. Not just nearby." He smiled grimly. "The cabin is one story. All the bedrooms are easily accessible. Yours especially because it's on the side closest to the forest. Easy in and easy out and the fact that it opens onto the wraparound part of the deck makes it an even more inviting target."

He finished his cappuccino and refilled his cup, his mind working like a computer, piecing what he knew together. He looked at me over his cup. "You were targeted specifically. You. Brynn. You're an only child and that makes you a great bargaining chip."

"I'm scared." It was the first time I'd said it out loud. Even to myself I sounded small and insignificant. I folded over and wrapped my arms around myself. My stomach roiled.

"Don't be afraid." He rose and came around to my

side of the table. "That's why I'm here. I won't let anything happen to you."

I felt the light touch of his hand on my hair and knew he meant every word. His hands slid to my shoulders and I shivered and didn't know if it was from fear of what almost happened or because Jace himself was so close and affecting me in ways I was too shook up to investigate though, if that was it, the feeling was surely magnified a thousand times by what had just happened. As I shivered I thought how it wasn't the first time Jace had affected me that way and not the only time I'd not known why. But this time was the most dangerous to my emotional health and physical safety.

As I stood there wrapped in Jace's arms I knew I must think about the two of us because we were like two vehicles careening towards each other without knowing whether to let the inevitable collision happen or sidestep enough to avoid it. I didn't know about him, but my feelings were escalating so fast that, forget about two vehicles, I was almost flying.

I decided I'd consider our situation when I had the time. Not yet. I'd do it when the drama was done and over with. When the immediate danger of the night intruder was no more. In the morning when the sun came up and I could look around and tell myself the world still existed and was normal and safe.

Then and only then would I think about me. And Jace. About us together. And about us not together. Because if there was one thing my father's talk with Jace had done, it was to make me face how I felt about him and what, if anything, I wished would happen. Or not happen.

I'd not tell Jace, of course, my thoughts would be my personal way of dealing with whatever I was feeling and would take into account both Jace himself and the situation we were in. I had no idea what I'd eventually think about us beyond that it would be completely weird because we were in a completely weird situation.

Except that little mental exercise with myself never happened. I never got around to considering any of it because when the sun came up and we went outside onto the deck to see if the intruder had left any evidence of his visit, we found the note and that blew everything else out of my mind

.

CHAPTER 12

Jace found it, actually. "What's this?" Did he see everything? Even a scrap of paper beneath a small rock on the table that was hardly noticeable?

He picked it up. He read it and his face went dark. "He never intended to kidnap you." He shoved the note in my direction. "Last night was a warning."

I read it out loud. "*I could have taken her if I wanted. If you don't give us the drug I will return and when I do I will take her and I will hurt her.*"

I dropped to the table, unable to remain upright. "I can't believe it." Somehow the note made what was happening beyond real. I'd accepted that I was in danger but reading the words took it to a whole new level. I started shivering so hard I couldn't see clearly, couldn't think straight, and as the seconds passed I grew colder. I folded over and wrapped my hands around my middle but it didn't help.

"Steady, Brynn." Jace moved close and draped a hand around my shoulder as he scowled in thought. "He must have put the note on the table before he came through the window because when I shot, he left as fast as possible. No time for dropping notes anywhere."

His arm didn't stop my shivering so he pulled me close and the sturdy warmth of his body lessened the shivering as he stared over the forest and thought more. "He expected last night's sneak attack to be easy but he learned otherwise. That means the note is meaningless because he now knows you're not an easy target."

His arms wrapped me closer, harder, and it helped but nothing could stop the shivering entirely. Someone wanted to do things to me. Bad things. Not because I deserved it, just because I was my mother's daughter and she had something they wanted. "Don't worry, Brynn. I won't let him get to you."

The next thing I knew we were kissing. I didn't know who instigated it or how it came about, just that we were together there on the deck and I drank him in because I needed the security he represented and because I needed the man himself. Then, without speaking, we separated and I looked up at him.

His visage was dark and dangerous, his body sturdy, his whole self on alert. He hadn't been like that before reading the note but he was then and that made him exactly what I needed. I said, "Thank you." For keeping me safe. For making me feel better. For kissing me.

Our looks connected. Then, as suddenly as the sun coming out after a thunderstorm, his dark and dangerous mien disappeared. I didn't know if it was a part of the professional bodyguard persona, or if he was putting on an act or reliving the kiss.

Whatever the reason, my shivering lessened and finally stopped as he grinned and said, "You're welcome." His face flushed ever so slightly as the grin grew and he half bowed. "Jace Browne, lovely lady protection specialist at your service. Currently under contract to Gaylord Peters to guard his most precious possession. His daughter."

The day and the world was sunny and bright and for a moment I knew nothing bad could happen. It didn't matter why he said it, why he grinned, why he held me like a broken doll. Jace Brown made me feel safe and I leaned against him and took his warmth into me greedily and eventually smiled along with him. Which I was sure had been his plan.

I turned and looked at the forest surrounding the cabin. The forest I'd grown up loving and exploring. In all those years, it had never seemed threatening. Now it did. "I don't think I'll go for a walk ever again." I found myself moving subtly closer to Jace if such was possible, which it probably wasn't. We were already stuck together like glue and I didn't care, I needed him. The strength of him. The confidence. The sense of safety he projected. He appeared not to notice me burrowing deeper and deeper into his body but I was sure he did.

"Good but not forever. For now, though, don't go anywhere alone. Stay close to the cabin. Real close. But if you should feel the need to take a walk because if you stay inside any longer you'll scream from being enclosed too long, I'll go with you."

I shook my head. "No walks at all until this whole thing is done." I shuddered and managed to pry myself infinitesimally away from him. At that moment my father's wishes for Jace and me and my own wishes for us were identical. We should be together. We were meant to be together. If he felt the same. Did he? Could he possibly?

"Everything will be fine as soon as your parents and Russell contract with some pharmaceutical company to manufacture the drug they discovered and I believe that's what they're working on right now." The thought was encouraging. "So a walk along one of those lovely trails in the woods could happen very soon."

But when my parents and Russell returned a few days later we learned it wasn't so simple after all. They talked over one another in a dizzying spate of words to let us know what was going on.

"Gaylord has a potential company to manufacture the drug."

"More than one, actually, but the field has been narrowed to a few."

"As soon as we have the rights to it from the tribe in the Amazon."

"We could barge into the Amazon with a ton of equipment and lots of brass and just start harvesting trees but I won't do that." My father pretended to cringe. "Your mother would kill me if I even suggested it."

My mother took over the explanation. "The thing is, if we're going to be decent people, there are two things that must be completed before we do anything.

"First we must have permission from the tribe that discovered the drug. They've been using it for hundreds of years so it's their drug.

"But it's more than the drug itself. It's how it's processed and no one outside of the tribe knows the details.

"The tribe must be a partner in the whole thing.

They should end up with the lion's share of the profits. And there will be profits."

My father smiled. "Lots of profits. Enough for everyone involved to be very happy."

Jace and I looked from one to another in total confusion as we figured they'd never stop talking over one another. I finally interrupted and asked, "So exactly what are you all trying to say?"

My father took over. As usual. "That we need to go to the Amazon and talk to the tribe. Show them the contract we worked out with Henry Torelle's help, though, per what Henry suggested, nothing is final yet. We arrange for them to have representation so they know what they are agreeing to. If they agree. If not we start all over.

"But if they do agree, then we ask them to show Abigail and Russell how they turn simple tree sap into something that wards off most diseases better than any vaccination or drug discovered so far."

"You're going to the Amazon?"

"As soon as we can make arrangements."

I remembered what had taken them to New York. "What about this Henry Torelle? Is he going too?"

"He's making arrangements with the pharmaceutical companies. We don't even know which ones because Henry, greedy person that he is, won't tell us. Yet. He wants to make sure we don't cut him out of the deal. He wants to make sure he gets his fee as intermediary."

My father shook his head and rolled his eyes. "He's one greedy guy, totally self-centered just as Russell said and I don't trust him as far as I can throw a bucket of bolts. So to answer your question, no, he's not going with us to the Amazon." He snorted. "He wanted to go. He hinted broadly. But I wouldn't let someone of his caliber near anything of value no matter what it is.

"But he knows the business of new pharmaceuticals. He's playing several companies against each other to get the most money. For him." He shrugged. "But that's okay as long as the end result is legal and binding and fair for everyone involved and there's no reason to think it'll be otherwise."

"What did the tribe say when you spoke to them?"

My father sagged. "I haven't talked with them yet. The Amazon isn't like New York. Yes, there is communication but it can be complicated. The tribe is modern but it's also a thousand years behind and it's both at the same time. But we're working on it and should hear from them shortly to let us know if we'll be welcome and if the tentative plan we've laid out is to their liking."

"And if it isn't?"

My father gave me a long look. "That won't happen. They'll agree."

Jace couldn't stifle his chuckle at that statement and our eyes met in complete agreement that my father was, indeed, a person who was used to getting what he wanted so of course the tribe would agree.

My father noticed our look. And smiled. Again! For what seemed like the hundredth time! And Jace and I went all stiff and formal and immediately turned away from each other until my father's attention wandered because we didn't want him to get the idea that he was about to get what he wanted. A son-in-law. Then we looked back and grinned like a couple of conspirators and I was glad we could laugh about our situation.

As I covertly considered Jace across the room, I realized that he and I did communicate via looks rather a lot. And smiles and frowns and sidewise glances and we used those things as much as words. I thought back to other people I'd known during my life and couldn't think of a single other person I'd shared so much with without saying a single word.

Was my father on to something after all? Was something special developing between Jace and me and my father had noticed it immediately? I discarded the thought as quickly as it appeared because, no, there was nothing going on, with the exception of the unusual circumstances we were struggling through, though my father did have the unique ability to sniff out secrets people didn't even know they harbored and our unusual situation gave rise to many.

Aside from our situation, though, I wondered if it was accidental that we were occasionally on the same wavelength that didn't require words. Or was it merely a thing that had come into existence because danger threatened?

By unspoken agreement – that special wavelength again – we didn't mention the attempted kidnapping or the note until the next day. The trio had arrived so hyped on the excitement of getting the new drug to the world that we couldn't dampen their enthusiasm immediately.

But the next morning after breakfast and the causal talk that always follows a meal, as the mid-morning slump began, Jace put his hands between his knees, coughed to get attention, and told them what had happened. And showed them the hand-written note.

From his perspective of years traveling through the rougher parts of the world, Russell nodded that, yes, this was the way things happened. My mother turned white and dropped into the nearest chair, unable to speak as she stared at me with wide, terrified eyes. My father pounded the table with his fist. "I knew it!"

"Knew what?" I hadn't the faintest idea which of the many things he could be referring to was what was in his mind.

"I knew Jace Browne was the man for the job. Think what would have happened if he wasn't around. If you were alone. Or with some other, less competent professional. You wouldn't be here today, that's what would have happened, because that intruder would have returned the next night and kidnapped you. Who knows where you'd be now. Tied up in some dungeon. Or worse." He pounded Jace's back. "Good man, Jace. Great job."

My mother rallied. "Yes." Her throat worked. "Thank you, Jace, for keeping Brynn safe."

Jace looked at them. "Brynn has a twenty-two rifle beside her bed. If I'd not been around, she'd have given a good accounting of herself."

"She has that twenty-two because you told her to keep it there."

There was silence for a long time. Then my father began pacing impatiently. Four steps in one direction followed by four steps in the other, hobbling because of the crutches but he'd learned to use them efficiently and they weren't an impediment. Back and forth. After a few rounds he stopped when he reached one end. He didn't turn. Instead his eyes narrowed as he looked at the computer screen directly in front of him with its revolving trail cam pictures of the forest.

"The trail cams helped. They told you someone was watching and you acted accordingly." He nodded approvingly.

Then his gaze turned from that screen to the huge plate-glass windows with their views of our surroundings from every direction and from every room. The cabin didn't have the dark corners of most log buildings because of those oversized windows and we could enjoy every change in the weather while eating or doing whatever we did at our favorite get-away spot. We'd all agreed they were one of the best features of the remodel.

Now my father pounded his fist into his other hand since there wasn't a table nearby for him to pound on. "The windows." He looked at Jace. "All that glass and you can't watch every single window while we are in the Amazon and who knows how long we'll be gone. Long enough for whoever is after Brynn to figure out the place is more vulnerable than usual. So Brynn will be in danger with just the two of you here."

Jace nodded. "Agreed. It's a problem."

My father looked him up and down. "Do you have a magical solution?"

"I don't do magic, so the answer is that I'll do the best I can."

My father's answer was muttered. "Which is considerable. But you're not a magician and while we're gone magic is the only thing that'll guarantee Brynn's safety in this cabin." He sighed mightily and gave the huge windows a baleful stare. "And all because we wanted sunshine."

I looked from one to the other, somewhat confused,

and Jace explained. "The windows let sunlight in. They can just as easily let a kidnapper in. All he'd need is a rifle butt to break one and he can simply walk through." He finished with, "And do whatever he came to do because I can't watch every window all the time."

He continued. "I stopped the kidnapper because he wasn't expecting trouble and when I confronted him, he left. Next time he'll be prepared. Probably have an accomplice."

"Oh." There was nothing else to say.

My father, however, wasn't finished. "That means Brynn is coming with us to the Amazon because we can't leave her here with only one person to guard her, even if that person is Jace Browne." His tone of voice said what he thought of Jace's abilities. He somberly looked Jace up and down. "So of course, as Bryn's bodyguard, you're coming too." He gave Jace a direct look. "Is your passport up to date?"

CHAPTER 13

Later, on the deck and doing nothing in particular, I asked Jace if he wanted to go to the Amazon or if he'd rather not. "No one asked you if you want to go. I'll talk to my dad if you don't."

"I'm okay with going. I hear it's exotic and I've never been there because the Army doesn't have a large presence in South America." He looked away but not before I saw a gleam in his eyes. "Actually I'm kind of looking forward to the Amazon. The jungle."

My mother looked up from whatever she was reading. A pharmaceutical magazine of some kind. "It's not a jungle. It's a rain forest but most people don't know the difference." Of course my globe-trotting mother knew. She probably knew each and every plant there, too.

Jace wanted to go. It was in his face. He was probably an adventure junkie. As for me, I wanted him to enjoy the trip. It was the least we could do for someone who'd changed their life to keep me safe. I said, "The good thing is no one will be looking for us in the Amazon so we should be able to relax. It'll be a relief."

He disagreed. "Don't think for a second you'll be safe just because it's remote. No place is safe from people determined to get what they want and I'm guessing the Amazon is the perfect place for a surprise attack. Or to hide bodies."

My face went white and I almost puked. "And here I was thinking it would be a vacation, both in the usual sense and as a vacation from staying alert twenty-four seven."

His eyes went soft, changing from the deep blue I was used to, to the lighter blue of a summer sky. I found the change fascinating as he reached close and touched my cheek gently. "You will be safe. I promise." Then we both looked towards my father to see if he'd noticed Jace's impulsive act. He'd have interpreted it as an intimate scene. A romantic interlude. But he hadn't seen us and we both breathed a sigh of relief as Jace's eyes turned once again the usual deep blue I couldn't get enough of.

When we went inside my father was on the phone talking to someone who was interpreting for someone else who knew someone who had something to do with the tribe that knew all about the immunity drug. It was a usual confusing business discussion. He paced as he talked, faster whenever the conversation grew complicated and slowing to a thumping stroll as things were worked out. I waited for him to either trip over the crutches or throw them away in disgust, but neither happened. When he shut off his phone he heaved a satisfied sigh and looked around at all of us. "It's settled. We're going to the Amazon. The tribe is expecting us. I'll see what flights are available."

Jace's eyes lit up. When we were alone again, in

the kitchen getting pop from the refrigerator, I asked him why. He already knew we were going so that wasn't why his eyes had gone bright at my father's last statement. He turned slightly red but he answered honestly. "I love planes. I love flying and the last leg of our trip will be in a plane small enough to land on a jungle airstrip."

"Didn't you say you have a pilot's license?"

"For prop planes, yes, and I fly every chance I get. Every kind of plane I can."

Arrangements had to be worked out to get to the tribe's home territory but that turned out not to be a problem. Everyone had current passports and my father knew someone with a corporate jet that was sitting at an airport doing nothing, so sooner than I'd have thought possible we were in that plane and on our way to South America.

My father explained the details of the trip as we climbed above the clouds in that awesomely luxurious jet. "We can't land at a small airport. They aren't built for jets. So we'll have to land at a large airport and transfer to a prop plane." We knew that much. He paused and looked around and added, "And then to canoes."

My mother and Russell just nodded because this was routine for the globe-trotting duo. It was new to my father and me. Jace merely watched the clouds beyond and far below the window and I had no way of reading his thoughts until he turned away from the scenery and our looks met. And he grinned. The man had a smile that could light up a room and he used it often. I liked that.

From our earlier conversation I figured he was

positively salivating over the small plane for the next leg of our journey and probably also over canoes and rain forests and whatever adventures we might encounter. Jace Browne belonged in an adventure movie.

I found myself grinning back while carefully turning away from my father because, after all, he already mentally had Jace and me going down the aisle together so I didn't want to encourage his fantasy further by actually letting him see the two of us sharing a smile. And the wedding and the isle was a fantasy. Absolutely. No doubt about it. Though why the thought was so depressing was more than I cared to consider.

After we landed and the jet was safely tucked in a hanger to keep it pristine for our return trip and for the owners' peace of mind, we transferred our luggage and ourselves to a smaller, prop plane that barely had room for everything and everyone.

Jace took the co-pilot's seat and he and the pilot spent the entire trip talking shop and becoming friends while the rest of us looked out the windows at the view below. I was used to the green forest of my childhood vacation home but this was different. It was alive, verdant and so dense it was impossible to know what lay beneath the spreading green canopy.

The canoes were even more cramped than the prop plane but in them we saw the Amazon up close and personal. No hand trailing in the water because you didn't know what might come up and bite it off. Avoid the branches that reached over the river because something might be on one and decide to drop down on you. And the sounds were utterly different from the forest I was used to.

It was so strange and fascinating that time telescoped and we arrived at our destination before I thought possible and I couldn't have said how far we went or how long it took because my mind had been on the scenery, not the time. But I'd forever remember that the birds were gorgeous and the cries of unseen animals sent shivers along my spine.

Jace's eyes flicked back and forth constantly though he gave the outward appearance of a relaxed tourist. I wanted to ask whether he was enjoying the scenery or watching for surprise attacks, except I didn't have to ask because I knew. He was on high alert, one hand hovering near the holster that held the Glock. But nothing happened and in due time we stepped onto the bank and then into the village of the tribe that had the secret to almost universal immunity.

Nothing got done the rest of that day beyond getting to know the villagers and the Amazon. We were shown everywhere and met everyone and since we relied on interpreters, when we went to sleep that night surrounded by mosquito netting I wasn't sure what had happened or what we'd said. I finally decided nothing specific had been accomplished but perhaps the most important thing of all – friendship – had been established. An assumption on my part but smiles are universal.

The next morning my parents and Russell got down to business with the village elders. As they settled down to discussions and negotiations, my father flicked a look towards Jace and me that said we were on our own. Of course, behind that look was the hope that we'd find someplace private and take our relationship to the next level.

Jace looked a cautious question at me. "Anything special you want to do?"

"A tour would be nice because I don't know anything about the Amazon but this place hasn't yet become a tourist mecca so no tour guides."

He looked around. "We can go for a walk. Keeping the village in sight, of course."

"Are you saying the great Jace Browne is capable of getting lost?"

He snorted. "More than capable in this jungle. And I don't care what your mother calls it, it looks like a jungle to me." He peered hard into the trees that ringed the village. "But I think I can keep us close enough to the village to not get lost." He grinned again, that grin I was coming to realize was an integral part of him. "Meaning we keep the village in sight at all times."

As we cautiously circled the village on trails I was reminded of the day we installed trail cams in the forest around the cabin. In both places we were surrounded by living things we couldn't see but the feeling here was peaceful. No people out to kill us in the Amazon.

The next few days were a repeat of that first day. My parents and Russell working out details of a partnership that would benefit everyone involved while Jace and I explored the jungle. Rain forest. Whatever it was called.

The villagers, realizing we were interested in the area, showed us a couple trails that we could follow away from the village without fear of getting lost and we meandered along them like the tourists we were, enjoying every single moment of what was a strange and mesmerizing place.

At home I could walk a fair distance from the cabin

and feel like I was in a different world. In the Amazon that happened three steps beyond the village. Just three steps and everything changed. Sounds were different. Louder. More raucous. And the feel of animals close by grew stronger the further we went from the village. But we never saw anything beyond the birds that were everywhere.

We tried looking for those invisible animals. We stopped at a branch in the trail we were on and turned around and around, seeking movement or anything that would be different from the flora. But we didn't know the area or the wildlife or what to look for so we saw nothing.

As we looked for those elusive animals, though, we inadvertently moved closer to one another. Close enough that we touched as we turned. Stopped. Backed away. Pretended nothing had happened and continued on as if we hadn't stopped.

We couldn't pretend for long, though, so we ended up inches apart and more and more aware of each other than I'd thought possible before the talk my father had had with Jace. We stood just so for a long time, silently, our breathing the only sound beyond the ever-present noisy birds.

I thought Jace would kiss me. He had that look in his eyes and I knew my own look echoed his. So I thought it would happen and it would be okay because my father was deep in discussions back in the village so he'd not know it was happening. If he didn't know about it and that sense he had about such things didn't kick in then we wouldn't have to worry about him at all.

But the kiss didn't happen. Instead, mini-seconds

before our lips met, we both pulled back and, without a word but knowing we were of one accord, we turned back the way we'd come and returned to the village, leaving me to wonder what it would have been like had we not stopped ourselves. Maybe next time? Or had my father's discussion with Jace killed any and all hope of such a thing happening? A real kiss with feeling.

Nothing happened the next day either because there was no walk along any of the paths. Instead, we packed our belongings and started the slow trip back to civilization. Some of us. My mother and Russell remained behind because the tribe promised to show them the process by which a simple tree sap became a medicinal miracle.

Jace and I sat close in the canoe on that return trip, watching as ripples spread across the water and became one with the current. In the prop plane Jace once more acted as co-pilot and he and the pilot talked like old friends after that first trip.

In the jet we sat across from one another as we looked out the windows and day-dreamed about the cloud formations. We moved awkwardly in our seats every time we stopped watching clouds and inspected the cabin and in general managed to ignore each other because my father was watching closely. For his sake we pretended we weren't overly aware of each other and most of the time we succeeded. Several times, however, our eyes met by accident and each time I saw in his eyes the same question I wondered myself. What that kiss would have been like if we'd let it happen.

CHAPTER 14

Jace's knowledge of security was why my father hired him. So of course, as we settled into my parents' apartment in New York once we'd returned from the Amazon, he asked for Jace's opinion. "I need to stay in the city to deal with Henry Torelle and whatever pharmaceuticals he's been in contact with. Abigail and Russell are still in the Amazon.

"That leaves you and Brynn. You can return to the cabin *if* you think it's safe and that's what Brynn wants. I'll be okay with it because I'll be returning shortly." He drew a deep breath. "The thing is, after that break-in I'm not sure if that's a good idea." His expression said he trusted whatever Jace would decide.

As he waited for Jace to answer, he turned to take in the apartment. It was large and comfortable and as secure as possible with restricted access and dedicated parking. But it wasn't as large as the cabin and had fewer rooms. Enough bedrooms, each with a bath, an office for my father and another for my mother but no deck, no patio, no forest to wander in and he knew those things were important to me. I loved him for caring enough to consider my wishes as well as my safety. He looked a question at Jase. "What do you think?"

Jace went to the window and looked down. "No way for anyone to get in from the street and Security questions everyone entering the building through the usual entrances." He tipped his head in thought. "No place is totally secure, but, yes, the apartment is the best bet for now even though it's confining for Brynn. When everyone is free to return to the cabin and there will be enough of us to cover all possible entry places, then the forest will be fine. Until then, there aren't enough people to watch all those windows and doors and the forest is as good as the Amazon for approaching a place unseen because not everyone uses paths to get somewhere. Trail cams don't guarantee safety."

My father nodded shortly. "I thought as much." He turned to me. "I know it's not what you prefer, Brynn, but it's for the best for you to stay here."

"Why not my own apartment?" My things were there. My furniture. My favorite snacks. It was home.

"It's not secure. Not like this place." I sighed. He was right. One of my favorite things about my apartment was the lack of people watching what I did no matter that their intentions were the best. There was no doorman. I'd thought that was wonderful. Until now.

I wasn't surprised that Jace agreed with my father but I sagged a bit as I accepted that I'd be stuck in this beautiful apartment without my personal things until my father could finish his business with whatever pharmaceutical would be creating the actual immunity drug. Not long, I hoped. A week or so. Maybe less.

Five days later he was still deep in discussions with Henry Torelle, who insisted on being the go-between and refused to tell him which pharmaceutical companies he was dealing with. Or how many. The man was infuriating.

"I'd fire him in an instant if he wasn't so good at what he does," was my father's comment that fifth day after storming into the apartment, ripping off his suit jacket and throwing it against the wall in an act of total frustration. "He's the greediest person I've ever met and he's afraid I'll cheat him out of a few pennies here and there if I talk directly with the people I'll be doing business with for the foreseeable future." He was disgusted. "The man is an insecure, suspicious piece of dog crap."

He raked a hand through his hair and poured himself a good slug of the whiskey he keeps for company because he doesn't drink except for special occasions. But he did that day. "I can see why Russell is happy to no longer be working with him. I can't imagine how he survived as long as he did."

He dropped into a chair and placed his empty glass on the coffee table before leaning back, looking out the window at the city view that was half the reason the apartment cost as much as it did and managed a small smile. "I'll be glad when contracts are signed and this whole affair is done and the world becomes the fortunate recipient of a drug that affords almost universal immunity to so many of the things that plague us now."

"Which is why you'll continue to deal with this Torelle person." Jace spoke quietly and my father nodded and I was glad Jace was there to say what I was thinking because I'd never have said anything myself with my father in the mood he was in.

With those simple words said when he knew my father would as likely throw a glass at him as agree with his statement my estimate of Jace Browne rose significantly and my admiration for him was already pretty high. Possibly in the stratosphere. His future wife, whomever she would be, would be fortunate.

Would she know how much of a gem she was getting? The thought intruded in my already over-full brain. I decided that if necessary I'd tell her. That was, I'd do so if Jace was still a part of my life when that day came. I might not be. We might have already gone our separate ways.

As I thought those thoughts and realized for the first time since I'd met Jace that, in the normal course of events, the day would come when he wasn't a part of my life, I felt a small but very sharp prick of unhappiness. I wished that kiss had happened in the Amazon so I'd have something to remember later. It would have been special among the luxuriant undergrowth. But it hadn't.

I couldn't sleep that night for thinking about that non-kiss and whatever might have happened afterwards that hadn't because the kiss hadn't happened. I sternly told myself to prepare for the day when he'd be somewhere else living whatever kind of life he wanted and I'd be doing the same in a different location. Because he was temporary unless my father got his way and that wasn't likely to happen because both Jace and I were determined not to let my father run our lives.

I was so busy thinking that I couldn't sleep. So I was awake when I heard a slight sound. I rolled over and listened. Maybe it was nothing. A distant car, perhaps, except the apartment was so well insulated that city noises didn't penetrate almost soundproof walls. Or the refrigerator making the noises refrigerators make. Except I knew that sound, too, and this one was different.

But there was a sound of some kind and as I listened I became more and more sure that it wasn't one that belonged. I reminded myself that I was hyper alert after the break-in at the cabin and was probably looking for danger where it didn't exist. Still, instead of closing my eyes and trying to return to sleep, I pushed the blankets aside and stopped breathing in order to hear better.

It came again. A scratching sound somewhere in the apartment. I couldn't place exactly where it originated but as I listened it moved and slowly approached the hallway to the bedrooms.

A person. Someone was in the apartment and they didn't want their presence known. Despite all the security someone had gotten in. Unless it was my father or Jace and they'd have no reason to be so quiet. A chill went along my spine as I sat up.

A light blinked. My cell phone. There was a text message. It was from Jace who of course was alert and in the next room. 'Get out of bed. Find the darkest part of your room and stay there. Don't open the door no matter what.'

I tapped 'okay' and hid behind the open door to the bathroom. Then I held my breath and wished he'd not said to stay in my room. I wanted to be with him. I wanted to conk someone over the head with something. Anything. I could do it, too, I could be brave as long as I was beside him.

I looked about in the dark room and grabbed the

only thing that remotely resembled a weapon because my twenty-two rifle was in the cabin hundreds of miles away. A chair. Lightweight and easy to pick up it wasn't much of a weapon but it was better than nothing.

I grasped it firmly and watched for the door to open. I was sure it would because the threats had specifically mentioned me and if someone knew enough to get in an apartment with top-of-the-line security then that person most likely knew which bedroom I used when I was there.

Then there was a different sound. The doorknob turning. I grasped the chair even harder and prepared to bash someone's head in.

The door started to open. Slowly. Silently.

Then all hell broke loose.

Lights came on, I heard a scuffle in the hallway followed by grunts and the sound of bodies scraping against the walls as I ran as fast as possible towards whatever was happening, my chair held like a cudgel.

I flew through the door and looked to see what was happening so as to best position myself to join the fray. But as I raised the chair high whoever had broken into my parents' apartment broke free of Jace's grip and ran. Down the hall through the living room and then through the open entry door. Then he was gone.

All I knew was that it was more likely a man than a woman and that guess was from the way the attacker moved instead of what I saw. I didn't know his race, whether he was large or medium sized, or what color hair he had because he wore a black outfit that covered him from head to toe.

Jace chased after him, plowing through the rooms at top speed but he wasn't fast enough. I heard running and then a door slamming. Then nothing. Jace returned, anger and frustration oozing from his every pore.

"He got away."

"You chased him away. That's all that matters."

"No it isn't." My father emerged from his room, fighting sleep and pulling on a bathrobe as he approached, thumping along on his crutches, and asked what was going on. Jace brought him up to speed in seconds. "He's gone but the fact that he disappeared so quickly says he had a place in the building to hide."

My father digested that information. "So he was in the building all along?"

"That's my guess." Jace nodded shortly. "Someone let him in earlier and provided a place for him to wait and when he ran out of here he returned to that place."

"Another apartment?"

"Possibly, but there are other places to hide and if I'm right there'll be no way to ever find out where he went or who provided that place."

My father examined the open door grimly. "This apartment isn't as safe as I thought."

Jace shrugged. "It's still a better bet than the cabin but judging by what just happened it's not a whole lot safer. Because no place is truly safe."

My father shut the door and shut the deadbolt that was now butchered. "This building is supposed to be secure. Every tenant is vetted, every apartment watched. Who could manage such a thing?"

"A professional." Jace led the way to the kitchen where we sat around the table because there'd be no more sleep that night. "Which is no surprise considering the amount of money involved."

My father nodded slowly. "Millions." He

reconsidered. "Not millions. Billions and more billions."

"Enough to make even the most expensive effort worth it."

My father would have dropped to a chair if he wasn't already seated. "This is way beyond anything I thought possible." He looked at Jace. "Are you still up to the job?"

Jace thought for a long time. "I'm still okay with our original deal. Protecting your daughter. She's one person and I can do that. But as for the entire situation, all of you and the immunity drug itself? It'll take more than one man."

There was silence for a long time. My father made coffee in the old-fashioned coffee maker my parents still used in their apartment, gulped a cup and poured himself still another one. He returned to the table and drank it quickly, breathing hard as it burned his throat. Then he set it down as if it was a gavel because he was ready to speak. "Where can I get reinforcements and what kind of reinforcements do I need?"

Jace thought for a few seconds. "You need to find out who's doing this. Then you need to convince them to stop."

"Easy to say but hard to do." Silence reigned again for long enough that we each finished the coffee we'd also drank and poured more and I started a second pot because we'd gone through the first one. But all the time we spent making and pouring and drinking coffee, my father was thinking.

"I'm going to hire a private investigator to find out what pharmaceutical firms are in the running for the drug. Both those going after it legitimately and those that don't care whether what they are doing is legal." He leaned his chair back on two legs. "So in the morning I'm going to start researching private investigators."

Jace cradled his cup in his hands as he smiled. "I may be able to help with that."

CHAPTER 15

"I have a friend," Jace began.

"From the military?" My father interrupted.

"Yes, but he's been out for a number of years."

"Doing what?"

"He's a private detective." My father smiled broadly as Jace continued. "From what I hear, he's a very good one. Has several PIs working with him and they have all the business they can handle, which says something."

"Think he'll fit us in his schedule?"

"We go way back. I'll call him as soon as the sun comes up and the work day begins."

Something in me relaxed a small bit. Someone had gotten into the apartment but now we had a plan. Call Jace's friend, hire him, find out who was trying to kill us, and stop them. Plus we still had Jace. Nothing bad could happen. I rose and stretched. "I'm going to bed."

"I thought you couldn't sleep."

"That was before. I think I'll sleep now." I moved

away from the table, put my cup in the dishwasher and headed for my bedroom and, yes, I felt safe even in the apartment because Jace was there and we had a plan.

"I'll do the same," Jace said softly.

"In the room next to Brynn's," my father added, just as softly. "Where even if you are sound asleep you'll hear if someone else decides to try where others have failed." He rose. "Just as you did at the cabin and again tonight. Or, even better, sleep in the same room. It's closer."

Jace and I exchanged glances, remembering our sleeping arrangements in the cabin. Now he dropped his cup into the sink and moved towards the living room as my father continued, "As for me, I'll watch the sun come up and, since I'll be awake, I'll be able to stop any would-be home invaders before they get through the door." He grinned. "I'll yell so loud Jace won't have to do anything because they'll have been scared to death."

The apartment was so many stories up that sunrises were possible even in the city, seen over buildings that would otherwise block the view. I'd never seen clouds through those windows but wouldn't have been surprised if some morning they appeared.

My father watched as Jace and I continued to the hallway where Jace had confronted the intruder. "Have a good rest of the night to you, Brynn. But not you, Jace, because I'm sure you'll stay awake even if I'm on watch."

Jace went slightly red. "I can take a nap later."

My father almost purred. "Spoken like a true professional who takes his job seriously." He fairly gloated over hiring the best man for the job as he poured himself still another cup of coffee and headed for the living room and those windows that weren't as large as the ones in the cabin but were more than enough to enjoy the sunrise that was already showing a few faint streaks of pink.

Jace moved his things and a mattress into my bedroom, wrapped himself in blankets and didn't sleep. I knew because as I lay in my bed and listened to his breathing it wasn't the even rhythm of sleep. Neither could I sleep though it was from Jace's nearness rather than fear. But somehow, eventually, I must have dropped off because the next thing I knew the sun was shining through those huge windows.

That day turned out to be disjointed. When I finally arose and made breakfast Jace was already up and looking somewhat the worse for wear. I took in his frazzled appearance. "You need sleep. I'm up, I'm fine, so you can get some rest." He started to object but his speech was interrupted by a yawn. I went to him and pushed gently on his chest. "Go. Rest. Sleep."

He flushed a bit as our looks met in a mutual agreement that this wasn't how we were supposed to act if we didn't want my father to get the wrong idea about us. We should be avoiding each other. But we weren't.

We were touching each other and acting in general like a couple, which made sense because as time passed we seemed to be getting closer and closer to each other. For reasons of safety only, not because we were getting closer any other way. Jace's feelings weren't changed. Mine were, I finally admitted, and they were changing even more with every passing hour. But I'd not admit it.

Then Jace yawned again even though he tried not to. He looked at my hand pushing on his chest, grinned, and went to our joint bedroom and shut the door.

I thought he was going to bed but he returned shortly carrying the Glock that seemed to be an extension of him. He handed it to me. "It's loaded. You're on watch while I sleep."

I examined the lightweight gun. "I'm not sure I could shoot anyone." I turned it over in my hands. "But if someone does break in I won't have to shoot because I'll scream the moment I see the door knob start to turn. You'll hear and come running. So I won't have to pull the trigger. I'll just hand the gun to you and let you do the shooting."

He had no retort. He didn't argue or grin or even comment in any way at all so I knew he was truly tired. And concerned. Our gazes connected one last time. Then I shoved him towards the bedroom for a last time and this time when he closed the door behind him it stayed shut.

My father, of course, had gone to bed long after the sun rose, leaving me the only one of the three awake and on watch with that Glock nearby. He and Jace both slept well past noon so it was late afternoon before all three of us were awake at the same time. Breakfast became an all day event as each of us rose in turn and headed for the kitchen.

My father, between bites of cinnamon bun slathered with butter, looked at the clock on the wall and said, "Too late to see your friend today, Jace." He turned to Jace. "Will you come with me tomorrow to talk to him?" Jace nodded, after which my father turned his attention to me. "You'll come too of course."

No need to ask why I was to come. The answer was obvious. If there was another break-in I'd be alone. I thought about the Glock. Maybe I should just ask to have it with me while I read a good book. Or not because of the question whether I could shoot another human being.

Not a problem if I didn't have to because there was someone else to do the shooting. Like Jace. If I was alone and feared for my life I might be able to pull the trigger. But I wasn't sure enough to stay in the apartment alone. "Of course I'll come. I've never met a private investigator. It should be interesting."

The next morning we got started later than planned. As we were about to leave my father's phone rang. He flipped it open and answered, somewhat irritated at the delay though his voice was as smooth as glass because over the years he'd trained himself to never sound irritated. It was a business thing. Never let anyone see you at less than the top of your game especially if the identity of the caller was in question and I saw by his quick glance, that there was no ID for this particular call.

He listened. Then he turned white. Then red with anger. Then he flicked the phone off and stared at it as if it was a snake about to bite. After several deep breaths to bring himself under control he shoved it in his pocket and said, "That was interesting."

We waited. If my father needed time to gain control of his emotions the call had been bad. He stood like a statue as he turned himself back into the consummate businessman he'd worked hard to become but he'd been sucker punched and it took a lot of willpower. "Someone thinks we should be afraid."

I pulled my father to the nearest chair because we weren't going anywhere until we knew what the caller had said. Jace followed, arms crossed and feet apart and waited. "That was last night's intruder or whoever hired him." I was blown away but Jace just nodded as if it was to be expected.

"Seems last night's break-in was just another sample of what will happen to us, like when they broke into Brynn's bedroom at the cabin. This call was for all of us and the caller made sure I understood that they'll harm any or all of us but that it was for Brynn especially. If we don't provide them with the formula for the immunity drug and agree not to manufacture it ourselves, bad things will happen to her."

Jace's eyes narrowed. "Does whoever called know you don't have the formula yet so you couldn't give it to them even if you wanted to?"

"They seem to think we have the whole deal sewed up and ready for production."

"Then they don't know everything. They aren't as powerful as they want you to believe." Jace thought furiously. His mind was racing. "Two things have been consistent in everything that has happened so far. The first thing is that they don't know much but are trying to make you think they do. The second thing is that they are threatening Brynn specifically because she's the most valuable thing you have. They'll attack anyone they can get close to if she's not available. Any target of opportunity but their preference is to take Brynn."

My father's voice was full of pain. "Brynn is our only child."

"And they know she's the one thing and probably the only thing that will make you give them what they want."

My father nodded miserably. "Brynn must be kept safe." His eyes sought Jace. "Your job just grew exponentially and so did your salary."

"The money isn't important." Jace was grim. "Keeping Brynn safe is all that matters."

My father nodded and then he sighed and rose but he moved like an old man as he crossed the room and hugged me. He was close to being broken and I knew I had to say something before he fell apart. "Don't stop what you're doing because of me. I'm not as important as the world getting the drug Mom and Russell discovered."

He draped an arm around my shoulders. "Yes you are, at least you are to me. You're my daughter, Brynn. You mother's and my flesh and blood. Even if we agree with you about the importance of this drug that doesn't change the fact that if you were kidnapped we'd not be able to stand by and do nothing. We aren't capable of letting you come to harm if we can prevent it. Asking us to do so would be asking for the impossible."

Jace agreed. "So, Brynn, starting today and until this is resolved you and I stick together like glue. I sleep in your room even if there's no obvious need for it. I go wherever you go. We will be joined at the hip so if you are grabbed they'll have to take me too and if that happens then what happens next won't be pretty."

He unfolded himself from the stance he'd been in ever since the phone call and moved casually towards the door. I sensed what he was doing. He was moving us past the call and into the future and he was doing so by physically getting us moving. "Remember our plan. Starting today we go on the offensive." He gestured for us to follow. "There's no time to waste so let's be on our way. We have a private investigator to chat with and a plan to formulate."

John Wilder Investigations filled the back rooms of an old brick building that screamed conservative values and dependability and old money. The room we were ushered into overlooked a small, elegantly designed yard that had been turned into a formal garden surrounded by a fence that gave it complete privacy. Jace's friend, John Wilder himself, glanced frequently out over that garden. I wondered if he'd enjoy visiting our cabin surrounded as it was by miles of forest. In a way that forest was merely a larger and more informal garden.

He listened without interrupting as my father and Jace explained the situation, nodding now and then while somehow still enjoying that lovely garden. I wondered if he'd remember anything they said. As I discovered shortly he remembered every single thing.

"I'll see what I can find out." He opened a computer, looked at it as if he hated technology and only used it when there was no other option, sighed, and began typing. Soon the screen was filled with every salient point we'd discussed along with names and all the details that went with them. "I think I have what I need but I might have questions as things progress."

Jace and John Wilder were good friends who hadn't seen each other in a while. That was evident and it was equally evident that they wanted to catch up with their lives but this was a work situation and they didn't want to impose their private wish on a client.

My father noticed. Of course he did because he noticed everything. He examined the garden John Wilder liked so much. "It's about lunch time." We waited to hear what he was working up to. "Do you ever have lunch out there? It's quite lovely." He went to the window. "I would if this was my place."

"As often as possible."

My father turned back to us. "Then what say I order something and we have lunch in that beautiful garden? You guys can catch up while Brynn and I simply enjoy being safe." He grinned slyly. "Can't get much safer than hanging out with a couple of former military types and that garden appeals to me more than a restaurant that's too open to chance eating there. Or the apartment someone broke into."

We had a wonderful afternoon because our time in that garden didn't end when lunch was consumed. Instead we were there for the remainder of the work day listening to war stories by Jace and John and learning the names of flowers I'd not known existed until then. John Wilder had planted each and every flower and bush himself during slow times when he wasn't chasing down fugitives and eliminating dangerous predators from the face of the earth.

When we left I admired how Jace's friend had replicated the country in the middle of the city and I wondered if all military types needed a place to go when life got difficult. Then I wondered further if my father's fixation on the cabin in the forest was his version of the same thing. A place to get away. A necessary retreat. An island of safety.

Until one day someone threatened us and it wasn't safe any longer. I prayed the cabin in the forest would once again become that idyllic and peaceful island. If so, it would be because of Jace and his friend.

And because we were now on the offensive.

CHAPTER 16

Before we heard from John Wilder Investigations we heard from my mother and Russell. "Come get us."

"That was fast. Can you replicate the drug already?"

"We're close enough to finish on our own but that's not the reason we want you to come. We need to get out of here and the sooner the better."

"Why?" My father went on alert.

"Things have been happening. Little things. Accidents in the lab, that kind of thing, but there are too many to be truly coincidental. Nothing deadly and no one has been harmed. Yet. But we are frankly concerned."

"Someone is trying to scare you?"

"If that's their intention then they are succeeding. We hope it's just a warning but if so the warning is getting more serious. Just the other day the batch we were working on smelled odd. When we tested it we discovered poison had been added. If anyone had ingested that batch they could have become ill. They could have ended up in the hospital. Or worse."

"Do you know who did it?"

"There's no way to know. This isn't a high security lab, it's a village in the Amazon. Anyone could have got to it."

"What about strangers in the village? It's isolated. The villagers would know if a stranger came through."

"It's not as isolated as it would seem. There's trade with other villages and boats that stop on a regular schedule with supplies and to bring friends and family here and carry villagers elsewhere for all kinds of reasons. Even a few tourists, the kind who want to get off the beaten path. The upshot is more people than we once thought."

"So there are too many suspects."

"I'm afraid so." My mother's voice turned hopeful. "But we now know the general thrust of the extraction method. We can figure out the details in a lab in the States."

"We'll be there as soon as I can make arrangements."

Arrangements didn't go as smoothly as for the first trip. The jet we'd borrowed was in use so we had to fly commercial and that slowed things down. After that flight the pilot of the small plane that we'd rented previously for the second leg of our trip was unexpectedly sick. We were already at the airport and preparing to board the plane when we got the news.

Fortunately the pilot remembered Jace and that they'd talked shop during the previous flight when Jace had been co-pilot. He decided Jace could take over as pilot. But it took time for Jace to map out where we'd be going and file a flight plan and for the airport people to make sure the arrangement was acceptable and legal.

We finally took off and after an uneventful flight

we landed on the same runway we'd landed on previously that couldn't handle anything larger than the plane we were in. On the return trip with two additional passengers and samples of the immunity drug we'd be stuffed in like sardines but Jace wasn't concerned. He pointed out that without the original pilot we'd actually have fewer people than for our first flight though the samples my mother and Russell were bringing made up for the lesser weight. Anyway, he said with a shrug as he arranged for the plane to be fueled and ready for the return trip, he'd get us home.

We thought we'd help my mother and Russell pack their lab samples and then we'd leave. It turned out not to be so simple because the villagers expected a visit from us and to leave immediately would be an insult. So it was two days before we could arrange for the trip home. Two days of smiling villagers interspersed with what I hoped would be private walks along those forested paths with Jace during which I also hoped for another romantic encounter. Maybe the kiss that hadn't happened the first time, followed by whatever might happen next. Nothing happened because the villagers accompanied us, smiling all the time. They didn't want us to feel ignored.

Early in the last morning, though, we did manage to get a brief walk. We sneaked out at dawn. By then we'd come to recognize some of the bird calls and walked quietly so as to hear them better and perhaps get a glimpse of them. We hid behind the greenery so as not to call attention to ourselves because we wanted to see and hear them.

So when two strangers to the village – perhaps they were tourists -- appeared they didn't see us. We watched them casually at first, the way people do who are people watching, between listening for the birds. We weren't surprised to see strangers in the village because my mother had been right that it wasn't as isolated as we'd previously thought but those tourists didn't normally use paths that weren't that clearly defined. The ones we did know.

Still, we didn't want company, not even if they spoke our language, which they did. I felt Jace's look and lifted my eyes to his and we both agreed silently that this wasn't why we'd come and we hoped the strangers would disappear soon and we'd encourage their leaving by not letting them know we were there so we wouldn't have to interact with them.

We couldn't make out their words until they grew close though the rhythm of the English language was unmistakable. But we wanted privacy so we hung back.

Jace was watching them and frowning in a way I couldn't read. He impulsively moved deeper into the shadow of trees that were draped with enough green stuff to form a curtain. He pulled me close and shushed me and I had the sudden uncomfortable feeling that his movement into concealment hadn't been impulsive after all.

I leaned my back against his chest so we could observe the newcomers though I still didn't see why he was so interested in them. But if Jace was interested there was probably a reason.

Jace's body was solid and warm and his heartbeat was steady and comfortable. I relaxed against him and enjoyed the feel of his arms around me and wished my father wasn't trying to match us for life because that wish meant we deliberately wouldn't let anything happen between us. We were both too independent to let anyone dictate our lives.

But I enjoyed the moment and the feel of the man and his arms as I absorbed the essence of him. Greedily. Totally. With every cell in my body. And I closed my eyes and dreamed. Until the two men came close enough that we could finally make out what they were saying.

"They're leaving today and they have samples."

"We can't let them get those samples home."

Jace's heart speeded up and his breath stopped for a moment as his arms around me tightened and we strained to hear better.

"We can't do anything. Too many people around."

"Can we destroy the samples before they leave?"

"Not possible with this tribe. They are as savvy as any New Yorker and twice as fierce."

"Then what do we do?

"I'll think of something."

They moved away. Jace and I stood for a few seconds in stunned silence. I turned in his arms to face him though I had nothing to say. But Jace's mind was working. "We need to get out of here before those guys figure a way to destroy what your mom and Russell worked so hard for."

"We can't let them see us. They'll know we overheard everything."

So we stayed on that trail until the strangers disappeared and for a long while afterwards. Jace kept his arms wrapped around me and my heart beat double time. But it was no romantic interlude, not any more. Instead, we were focused on getting back to the village.

Jace fumed at the delay and even as he held me he

was thinking what had to be done to get away quickly. He mentally organized our leave taking. "Are the canoes ready? What about the guides? Are they even up yet? Is our gear by the river or do we have to carry it there?"

When we were sure the men were gone we hurried to the tents where the rest of our group was staying. After a quick explanation we were all up, packed and ready to go. My mother and Russel, being the most familiar with the tribe, explained through an interpreter that there was an emergency and we needed to leave immediately.

The tribe bought it. I felt no guilt at our deception as we began the canoe trip to the small airfield where the plane awaited that Jace would fly to get us to the larger airport and a commercial flight home. I'd not relax until we were on that flight. Maybe not even then.

Jace muttered in my ear as we glided along the Amazon in those canoes. "I hope those guys don't know we're gone. I hope we have a good head start because if they are as serious as I think they are they'll be after us and canoes aren't bullet proof." I remembered what he'd said about the Amazon being a good place to hide bodies and wondered how easy it would be to sink canoes with the occupants still in them.

We had no way of knowing how many villagers had seen us leave or what they'd said after we'd left. Had they talked about us? Had they gossiped about our abrupt departure? If so had those strangers overheard them? Did they know the language well enough to know what the villagers said?

How much trouble were we in?

In spite of our concerns, though, the first leg of our trip home was quiet and uneventful. The birds were the only noisy things in that green forest that was a veritable orgy of luxuriant growth. But the only thing that mattered was how fast we could get to that small plane so Jace could get us out of there.

The canoe trip went surprisingly quick. The paddlers must have sensed our hurry and so they got us to the short walk to the airstrip in less time than before. Our luggage was unloaded efficiently and transported to the airstrip where it was loaded onto the plane that was waiting and fueled. We piled in and strapped ourselves securely and I cautiously began to breathe easier as the engine revved and the propellers roared into action.

Then there was a commotion just beyond the small airstrip. Two men had arrived and were arguing with the men who'd gotten our plane ready who weren't agreeing to whatever the newcomers wanted. I saw them shake their heads decisively several times. But the newcomers didn't leave.

Instead they pushed the airport personnel aside as if they were nothing and advanced towards us. Then I saw what they were carrying. Guns, rifles to be exact, the kind that make audiences shiver in action movies. Large, black, and deadly. And the men carrying them were headed towards us.

"Jace!" I pointed, but Jace had seen them and was already checking the gauges on the plane's dashboard.

He shouted. "Make sure you're strapped in." The engines roared higher, harder and the plane began to shake as it readied for takeoff as Jace's look skipped from the gauges to the advancing men and back until with a wave he indicated the chocks be removed and we started to taxi to the main runway.

But the men with the guns were coming faster than we were taxiing and as they came they raised those wicked looking rifles and aimed them at us.

"Duck!" Jace yelled as we reached the runway and turned into the wind. The engine's roar shifted to a higher pitch and we began moving down the runway as fast as Jace could make the plane move.

But the men with rifles were still coming. I couldn't hear the shots for the sound of the engine but I knew they were shooting because Jace began swerving back and forth on the runway, making the plane a difficult target. But the men kept coming. And shooting.

Jace didn't wait to take off until we reached the end of the runway. Instead, as the engine roared louder and still louder, the small plane suddenly and with a shudder lifted off the ground and went airborne. Our climb was so steep I didn't think it would hold together and the small plane shuddered under the strain as the men on the ground chased after us.

A hole appeared suddenly inches from where I sat. Jace swore quietly and pushed the small aircraft still harder and I prayed we'd not stall and that no more bullet holes would pierce the skin of the plane.

And then, miraculously, we were beyond the airport and any possibility of bullets reaching us. I knew the instant we reached that point because Jace relaxed. Not a lot but enough to know we were safe.

"Look for more holes," he told us.

We did as he asked and found several. A couple might have hit one of us if our luggage hadn't stopped them. But we were alive and unhurt and the plane was flying. I leaned back and closed my eyes and sent a prayer of thanks skyward. Because we were safe.

I didn't watch the scenery on that trip. Not the wispy clouds or the green forest beneath. Instead I found myself watching Jace. No scenery could compete with the play of emotions that crossed his face. Elation that we'd made it. Fear for what could have happened. Anger at the men with guns. Frustration that we'd had to deal with them. Pride in his ability to get us to safety. A dozen emotions crossed his face at one time or another during that trip.

As the miles passed, though, another emotion appeared. Concern. As I watched he glanced more and more at the gauges and each time his concern grew. Until he said, "They hit the fuel tanks. We won't make it."

In the back seat my father shrugged. "So we'll land at a closer airport and rent a car." Worst that could happen was we'd have to take a later flight home.

Jace's reply sent cold chills along my spine. "There are no closer airports."

CHAPTER 17

The Amazon below stretched green and unbroken as far as we could see. No airports. No highways. Just miles of tall trees growing so close together that we'd not hit the ground when we ran out of fuel, we'd hit trees instead. But those trees would tear us apart just as well as rocks and dirt. Survival was unlikely.

"There!" Jace pointed and I saw a brown slash in that carpet of green. "A plantation or something similar." Soon we were circling the brown area and, yes, it was an area of ground instead of trees. Less room than the small airport the plane had landed on before but it was better than nothing.

Russell peered at it from the back seat. "The Amazon is being deforested as fast as developers can cut the trees." He peered at it carefully. "And for the first time in my life, I'm glad of it." He used binoculars to see better. "It must have been cut recently because it's rough. Branches and detritus everywhere. Not to mention that it's not large." He gave Jace a questioning look. "Can you do it?"

Jace had been examining the cleared area as he circled lower and still lower. "Of course I can," he said in a voice that couldn't conceal his concern. "Anyway, small as it is, it's our best bet." He forced a cheerful note into his next words. "This is a good plane. Nice and maneuverable. Besides I can fly anything." Then he shrugged so elaborately it had to be an act. "Piece of cake."

Thinking over what he'd just said he added, "But make sure everything is tied down, make sure you are strapped in, and bend over as low as possible because it's going to be a crash landing." His pretend grin didn't fool any of us. "Just a precaution."

From the sky the brown slash had looked like the answer to a prayer. Up close it seemed more like a nightmare of rough ground, tree stumps and the remains of logging everywhere. Jace circled several times examining the ground and the detritus as he mentally measured the distance we'd have to travel once we hit the ground but it was impossible to read his thoughts. Then, with a brief nod that said he'd figured out the best place to land he turned the plane one last time and ever so slowly nosed it down.

"Brace yourselves!" He yelled in a hoarse voice and we bent over and grabbed whatever we could find as I realized with a sinking feeling in my stomach that, as the pilot, Jace couldn't do the same.

We hit the ground. Hard. But the first second was okay. We were down and in one piece. Then, as the plane slowed with Jace braking hard we hit the brush that hadn't been removed when the trees were cut. We bounced back into the air and then came down a second time with a thud that shook my teeth.

The plane turned part way around, flipped slightly and slid sidewise into a pile of brush. I had a glimpse of branches pressing against the window trying to penetrate the glass and seeming to slide past as we slowed. Then an especially large branch hit the window and it broke and those branches were in the plane itself and pummeling us.

I ducked lower and put my hands over my head and hoped Jace could do likewise while knowing he couldn't. Then the pummeling stopped and silence reigned. I looked up and those branches were thick around us and filling every space in the tiny plane as if growing there.

It was like being buried in a green thicket. The clearing had been done so recently that the leaves were still green and healthy. Most of all, though, they'd been thick enough to slow the plane and cushion it from the worst of the brush.

I cautiously raised my head and looked ahead to where we'd be if those leaves hadn't stopped our headlong rush. What I saw made me give thanks because there was no way we'd have survived crashing into the pile of logs mere yards ahead.

Jace dropped his head to the steering wheel and stayed that way for a long time. Then he sat up straight turned to the rest of us. "Everyone okay?"

We were all functional. A bit of blood here and there from the branches that littered the plane's interior but otherwise we were unharmed. "No broken bones, no major injuries," was Russell's cheerful assessment as if crash landings were an everyday occurrence. "So now what?"

Jace and I almost didn't hear his question. We were staring at one another. Never mind that my father was in the back seat watching. Never mind that he was trying his best to orchestrate a match between us and that we were determined not to let him dictate our lives and that meant ignoring each other.

The only thing that mattered at that moment was that we were both alive. Jace took my hand and we sat that way for a long time silently communicating in that way we'd developed and telling each other without words or even looks that everything was okay. That we were both safe.

And somehow without words or even looks we also communicated how foolish we'd been to not acknowledge what was developing between us because what if this had been the end and we'd not told each other how we felt because of a silly need to assert our independence. As we sat there with our hands intertwined I realized that what was between us was special. So special that we didn't need words. And that was how it had been with us from the very first.

Russell's voice penetrated our bubble. We dropped hands and Jace turned to those behind us and answered Russell's question as to what was next. "We figure how to get to civilization, that's what's next."

The answer proved both easier than expected and harder.

As we started slowly to assess the situation and try the plane doors to see if they could be opened I saw movement from the corner of my eye. I gestured to Jace and realized that he, too, saw the figure that was approaching but was still too far away to know anything about who or what it was. Just movement. Someone or something coming towards us.

My parents and Russell also saw the figure and stopped trying to open the doors. In dead silence we waited for what was about to happen. Because, as Jace said almost in a whisper, "This cleared area is undoubtedly illegal. So that man coming as fast as he can run must also be illegal."

"Not to mention that he's carrying a wicked looking rifle," was my father's dry addition to the conversation.

"Out of the frying pan and into the fire." My mother looked my way. I knew what she was thinking. That after all the care they'd taken they gotten their only child into a dangerous situation. I wanted to assure her that I was an adult and wouldn't have had it any other way but before I could speak our visitor reached the plane, rifle loaded and pointed straight at us.

We started to climb out with our hands in the air. But the brush against the doors prevented us from opening them. The man with the gun muttered in frustration and then helped with one hand while holding that wicked looking rifle with the other. When we were all out of the plane he used the rifle to gesture for us to stand in a line. Then he paced back and forth in front of us, inspecting us. We had no idea what he was looking for.

He spoke. His words were in Spanish so none of us knew what he was saying. My father started to take a step forward but stopped instantly as the man shoved the rifle into his stomach. He backed up and remained quiet.

Jace spoke. "We're Americans. We don't speak Spanish." He waited for a response but got none though it was clear the man got the gist of what he was saying. He bit his lower lip and then gestured again with the rifle indicating we should walk in front of him and pointing with it to a shack in the distance.

We walked, hands in the air except for my father who was still on crutches. No one said anything. Soon we reached the shack where a few men stood around doing nothing. One man, though, seemed to be the leader. Our captor strode to him and they spoke in Spanish. Then the leader turned to us. "Americans?"

Jace answered. "Yes. We ran out of fuel. We had to

land and this was the only cleared area."

The leader grunted. Then he spoke in English. "I don't believe you. No reason to run out of fuel. You're with the authorities." He smiled without humor. "I don't like the authorities."

"We were shot at. The tanks were hit and we leaked fuel."

The man frowned. Then he snapped his fingers and spoke to the men standing around. Two of them took off towards the plane at a half run. Jace said quietly, "I think they are going to check. I'm sure they'll find holes in the fuel tanks."

We waited for their return in that cleared area close enough to the forest that we could reach out and touch it but where we stood in that sun we felt the full heat of the day. Our captors lounged in the shade of the shack but every time we moved a rifle followed our movements. So we stood in the sun and baked until the two men returned.

They spoke to their leader and he turned to us. "You told the truth. There are bullet holes in your tanks." He looked Jace up and down. He recognized Jace's military background. Was that good or bad? "Why do you have bullet holes in your tanks?"

Jace thought a moment. Then he cautiously told the leader a skewed version of recent events. He left out the bit about the immunity drug that was still in the plane. Instead he said we were a group of tourists who'd visited a remote tribe for a vacation and some thugs had decided to steal from us. He said he was our pilot and that we'd barely gotten away.

It was a good story. It could have happened that way. The leader's gaze shifted from Jace to my father and looked him up and down for a long time. "Who are you to be worth stealing from?"

"I'm Gaylord Peters, that's who I am." My father's chin went up in his best Chairman of the Board pose as he explained to the leader just who he was and what he did for a living. Which was complicated because he bought and sold companies and negotiated deals to connect still more companies with each other. But somehow he got the idea across. He was a big-time businessman.

The leader smiled and this time it was as genuine a smile as possible considering he held a rifle aimed at us. He poked the rifle at my father but as if it was a joke "You and me, we are alike, I think." He laughed and moved the rifle to a more comfortable position. Away from us. "We do whatever makes money, right?"

My father nodded agreement. No reason to mention that he worked within the law and our captor clearly did not. As we broiled under that sun our captor looked us over still another time and then unexpectedly leaned the rifle against the shack. "So how badly do you want to get home?"

I saw it in my father's eyes. They were two businessmen about to negotiate our return home. The only question was how much would it cost and could we sneak the immunity drug into our luggage without them finding out about it and charging even more because we had it. Because if they knew what it was and what it was worth they'd keep it for themselves and end our lives.

In the next few minutes my respect for my father increased exponentially as I discovered how truly exceptional his business skills were. He managed to negotiate our safe transport to the airport by truck because that was all the transportation available and we'd have to sit in the back in the sun. t

But somehow, amazingly, he also arranged for us to bring our luggage – all of it – in that truck. Because we had sentimental keepsakes, he said, nodding to my mother and me and rolling his eyes as if we were a couple of pampered society women who'd complain if we didn't have our knick-knacks. He managed to make the luggage seem important, just not in the way it truly was.

So about the time I thought we'd pass out from the heat we were brought into that shack and given water to drink. Then my father got on a computer in a corner and arranged for the transfer of a huge sum to the leader of the small group of thugs. A really huge sum and worth every cent.

When he got off the computer we returned to the plane and without the help of those men who'd been told to retrieve our luggage we got everything that was important into the back of a truck. We were careful.

They never saw how we packed and were more than happy to let us carry everything ourselves. They thought we were afraid of them and were pretty sure their words among each other was about how we were doing the work their leader had ordered them to do and weren't they clever to have us do their job. Load our own luggage.

We didn't enlighten them as to why we didn't complain. When we were done the immunity drug was safely packed between slacks and shirts. Then we climbed into the back of the truck and left with a promise to be on time for our flight.

CHAPTER 18

I breathed a sigh of relief when we were finally at the airport and had gone through security and were in the air. "I don't like to fly," I admitted to Jace as he enjoyed the scenery and, unlike me, didn't appear to suffer any lingering effects from almost dying in a plane crash or from almost being shot.

He blinked in surprise. We were seated next to each other. Of course we were. My father had arranged for the flight and also the seating. Now he beamed at us from a few rows back, proud of his carefully orchestrated interference in our lives.

Jace, ignoring my father, took my hand. "This plane is safe as a baby's crib."

"If you were the pilot I might agree."

"I don't fly jets." Jace examined our intertwined hands. Then he did something unexpected. He put one arm casually around my shoulder.

I knew what he was doing. Making me feel safe. "Be careful what you do, Jace. My father is watching."

"You know what?" He spoke in a voice so soft it

was barely more than a whisper. "He can think whatever he wants but it won't change what I do." That arm dropped lower and wrapped me as close as possible considering we were on a plane and had an armrest between us.

He turned towards me. "If he gets the wrong impression from seeing us together then that's his problem and not mine. On the other hand maybe he's getting the right impression."

I couldn't breathe for a moment as he continued. "Furthermore I've made a decision and I think you have too." Yes, we'd communicated silently when we were alive after the crash landing and, yes, I'd been pretty sure he'd thought the same as I did. That we were foolish to hold back our feelings because of my father.

"I don't intend to let what he's thinking stop me from enjoying your company. From enjoying you. Not anymore. Not ever again." His hand turned my head towards him and there was something in his eyes, a depth I'd never seen before. I was literally incapable of speech.

His voice took on a deeper timbre. "We could have died back there. I'm never again going to waste time worrying about what other people think, not even your father." His arm wrapped tighter around me and I found myself leaning into him and not just because I didn't like flying. I couldn't have stopped myself from moving closer no matter how hard I tried.

We eventually got back to the States and to my

parents' apartment where we spent a few days while my father touched bases with Henry Torelle. Days during which my father couldn't stop smiling beneficently while Jace and I pretended not to notice and my mother and Russell asked each other what was going on. Why was my father smiling so much? And what did it have to do with Jace and me because obviously it did.

They asked me what was going on but I said I didn't know. They knew I was lying because I'm a terrible liar but they never did get the truth out of me. Or Jace. I mean, how many people are willing to admit someone is trying to get them together with someone else and to also admit that they are suddenly okay with the idea?

So with no information about my father's ever-growing smiles they talked about Henry Torelle instead. Russell had refused to have anything to do with him once he'd gotten him together with my father and when my father returned from one of his visits with Henry he told Russell he understood. "I'd not talk with him either if I didn't need him."

He shrugged out of his suit coat and slumped into the nearest chair. Then he stared out the window for a long time without seeing a thing. "But you were right that he has the pulse of the business. No one else could do what he's doing. I just wish he wasn't so secretive about everything."

He struggled upright to take the cup of coffee my mother had poured. "I'll be glad when this whole thing is done with and we can get back to a normal life." Then he looked at Jace and me. "The new normal that is. I expect it'll be different. In a good way. I hope." His face was blank but his eyes were calculating shrewdly. Were we a couple yet? He clearly thought that if we weren't yet, we were close.

I hoped Jace was ignoring that look. Could my father's obvious interest in our potential love life doom us as a couple in spite of what Jace had just said? Could his over-the-top interest have the effect of pushing Jace into deciding that he wouldn't let my father dictate his love life? It could happen despite the way the crash had thrown us together. I hoped not but I privately admitted that my father's well-meaning attention could doom the very thing he hoped to accomplish.

I didn't want that to happen so I stared daggers at my father. He responded with a broad smile as he leaned back happily and stared nonchalantly at the ceiling. When my mother brought him another cup of hot, black, coffee he downed it with a pleased expression and I wished I knew whether that expression was because he liked coffee or because he was satisfied with the way his meddling in the life of his daughter – me – was progressing. Or was it because the immunity drug would soon be in a research facility? Too many possibilities. I wanted to hit my head against a wall in frustration.

Three days of binge watching The Office later he had things in order enough that we all packed and headed back to the cabin though nothing had been done the way he preferred. He made sure we understood that. "Henry Torelle is a greedy idiot. If he didn't know everyone in the pharmaceutical business I'd kick him from here to Sunday."

He scowled at the mere thought of being bested by Russell's former partner. "But he does know the business and he made it more than clear that he'll do the negotiating, not me, at least until the major points are worked out. Then and only then will I be allowed to know where my money is going." He shook his head and muttered, "I'm not as good as I thought. I'm being bested by an idiot."

None of us said anything but it was hard to keep from laughing, especially Russell, who said, "I told you so," before looking at us and giving a sigh of contentment. "Now to enjoy your luxurious so-called cabin in the forest that I visit as often as possible in order to indulge in the kind of life I'd hate on a day-to-day basis but do enjoy between pharmaceutical treasure hunts with my excellent partner." He cocked an eye at his partner. My mother.

She nodded because finding new drugs was their shared passion, something my father and I had long ago accepted. My mother was the daughter Russell had never had, the person he hoped would carry on his legacy and we didn't interfere with that unique relationship.

The first morning back at the cabin Jace laid out

the rules. "No one leaves the cabin without telling me first and then only if accompanied by me and a couple of rifles." He continued, keeping one eye on the person the speech was for, Russell, whose visage grew darker with each rule because he didn't like being told what to do.

"We post guards at night. The security system at the cabin is excellent but all it does is tell us if someone is here and then only if we happen to be watching the cameras." His look sparred with Russell's, the man who didn't believe anything could ever go wrong. "So we take turns monitoring all those cameras during the day and standing watch all night long."

"Why stand watches? Aren't the trail cams enough?"

"They're no good at night. Not good enough for me." Russell frowned because while we heard common-sense rules for staying alive our globe-trotting explorer and discoverer of exotic drugs heard Jace telling him how to live his life and he didn't like it any more than Jace and I liked my father telling us how to live ours. But he was polite enough to only say, "Sounds like malarky to me."

He heaved a huge and totally fake sigh. "But it's your cabin, Gaylord." Then he turned to Jace. "And your rules." He finished with, "So be it." His polite words didn't fool any of us. The globe-trotting discoverer didn't like the rules and we could only hope he'd follow them. With his history of going everywhere and doing everything with no regard for the consequences that was doubtful.

The first two days were fine. Russell took his turn monitoring the security cameras during the day and standing watch at night. He enjoyed the ever-changing scenery as the monitors switched from one tail cam to another and gave him an over-view of the forest I'd known all my life that he'd never truly gotten to know because he'd never stayed long enough to explore the surrounding woods.

He'd always been between expeditions when he visited the cabin and had always been more than happy to merely relax on the deck with something to drink instead of replicating the hard treks that searching for new drugs seemed to involve. Plus he was getting older. Those exotic places were more and more of a physical challenge for his aging body and the cabin was a comfortable place to recharge with soft beds, warm sun, and ice cold tea.

Then one day while watching the trail cams he saw something that caught his interest. "What's that?" He pointed to the monitor but it had already moved to the next camera. "Can you go back?"

"Did you see someone?" Jace was instantly alert.

"Not someone. Something." Russell went towards the computer and would have started flipping switches and turning knobs if Jace hadn't gotten there first. As Jace protected the equipment Russell turned to my mother. "Did you see it?"

"See what? I didn't see anything." My mother joined us as Jace fiddled with the computer until it returned to the recording that had interested Russell.

Russell jabbed a finger at the picture. "That." His voice rose in excitement. "That plant." He turned to my mother. "What do you see? It's got potential, don't you think?"

She examined the recorded picture. "It's a barberry plant." She shrugged. "They are not uncommon around here."

He jabbed harder at the monitor. "I know but barberry is red. The berries on that bush are purple. Almost black." He stared at her, willing her to follow his thoughts. "Purple. That deeper color should indicate more medicinal qualities."

My mother tipped her head in thought. "Barberry is antiseptic. So I suppose purple should increase its antiseptic properties. But it's not a miracle drug."

He shook his head in exasperation. "Doesn't have to be a miracle drug. Just a better antiseptic and that's worth checking out." He stared at the plant as if it had secrets to share. "Where exactly is that trail cam located?" He moved towards the door. "I want to see that plant for myself." He fairly danced with impatience and opened the door on his way to somewhere even though he didn't know where to find that plant once he was outside.

"Slow down," Jace blocked his path. "Not now." He glanced at the sky. "It's almost night and that camera is rather far off. If you go now it'll be dark by the time you reach it." His eyes narrowed as he took in the elderly man who'd never listened to anyone in his entire life and wasn't about to listen to Jace now. "The rule is that no one goes running off into the forest alone. Remember?"

Russell looked for someone who'd help him stand up to Jace. All of us stood firm against his going into the forest. "I want to see that plant. I need to see it."

Jace showed Russell on a map where the trail cam with the barberry plant was located. Russell, with his experience, went to the door and stared at the forest, nodding when he'd figured out where in the real world he could find the plant he wanted to check out.

Then he and Jace tried to stare each other down because Russell wanted to go and Jace didn't want him to. Neither succeeded but Jace finally relented and said, "Tomorrow. After breakfast." His folded arms and spread-apart legs said Russell wasn't leaving the cabin and the elderly man finally caved. "Furthermore, when you go I go with you."

"Okay." "But he didn't like waiting. "Tomorrow. After breakfast. Immediately after." He stuck his head towards Jace. "If you are late I'll go alone."

Jace nodded. "Good enough. You and I can check out the – what did you call it?"

"Barberry. It's a medicinal plant. Both the berries and the roots are good for you."

"Barberry. We'll go tomorrow and bring samples

back."

My mother spoke. "I have minimal lab equipment here. Nothing major but better than a kids' chemistry set. We can check out any samples you find." Because it would be something to do, a way to keep Russell happy.

Russell relaxed back to his usual self and the rest of the evening was spent watching the sun go down and the stars come out and spread across the vast expanse of sky that we'd never seen when the cabin had been hidden beneath the trees but showed in all their glory from the deck that had been part of the remodel that continued across a slight hill to one side of the cabin.

The nicest thing about that deck that was designed specifically to view the sky, the part I'd not thought about when it was built but appreciated that night, was the several niches that had been built into it to guarantee privacy while viewing the night sky.

Jace and I somehow found ourselves in one such niche lying back on the heavy wooden lounges covered by thick pads that allowed watchers to view the sky in comfort. After a few minutes Jace left his lounge and joined me on mine, gently shoving me to one side to make room for himself. He didn't say anything, he just came and the next thing I knew his arm was beneath my shoulder and together we inspected the stars and the rising moon.

He spoke quietly, pointing to a streak across the sky. "A shooting star." He went quiet again as I nodded against his warm body to indicate that I'd seen it. "Or space junk burning up on reentry."

"It wasn't junk. It was too lovely to be junk. It was a shooting star." We were quiet after that, looking for another shooting star, but none showed. Then without warning he pulled me close, rolled me towards him and kissed me.

It was the kiss we hadn't had in the Amazon and after all we'd been through getting home it was way more than that kiss would have been. Long and slow and somewhere between light and passionate as kisses were rated. It was comfortable and sizzling at the same time. A perfect practice kiss.

Our second kiss wasn't light or comfortable at all. Not even close. Or our third or fourth. Eventually we lost count and simply lay beneath the stars and learned about each other and everything I learned made me want to know more as I decided my father's wishes were irrelevant. What he wanted had nothing to do with what was happening that night. It was all Jace and me.

Then my mother called everyone together and said we'd best get some sleep if Russell was to find that barberry plant the next morning and we returned to the cabin and our bedroom. Jace was in my bedroom, of course, on the floor beside me. Just in case.

It was difficult after those kisses. After being close to him. After taking the next hesitant step towards whatever would happen between us.

I listened to him for a long time as I lay there in the

dark thinking about him while knowing he was thinking about me and we remained chastely apart. But eventually sleep took over as it always does. Besides, Jace was scheduled take the next watch and needed what little sleep he could get.

Later, as I heard him slip out of his mattress on the floor and head for the deck to take his turn keeping everyone safe I wished he was in bed beside me instead of just close but knowing where he'd be made me believe nothing bad could possibly happen. So I rolled onto my side and slept.

CHAPTER 19

I awoke late the next morning to the sound of Jace in the next room where he kept his clothes and got ready for each day. I pictured his movements. The first thing would be to check his Glock. Of course. That was followed by time in the bathroom then I'd hear him rummaging through the closet then I'd hear the door close as he dressed for the day. Jeans, of course, as we all wore at the cabin.

I smiled as I remembered how well those faded jeans fit. The man was a walking advertisement for a fitness club. Or the military. Or saving peoples' lives. Thinking about him getting ready for the day drove me to do the same but I was in no hurry so I dawdled in front of the mirror and in the shower. We had all day. Perhaps, I thought as I contained my still damp hair in a pony tail, Jace and I had the rest of our lives. Was that possible? It began to feel that it was. Maybe.

We'd not said anything last night, we'd hardly spoken at all because we were busy doing other things but life was definitely going in the right direction. I sternly told my mirror self not to put too much importance on a few kisses because, after all, it had been a starry night and people do foolish thing beneath the stars. Besides, we'd been through a lot. We'd needed to unwind. So I shouldn't read a future into what was happening between us.

For that matter, we weren't out of danger yet but I was confident that with Jace in charge of security and my father working the business angle everything would come together soon as my mother and Russell finished their work in the lab. Then we'd see what the future would look like.

I tried to imagine that future but all I could come up with was Jace and me together. Hopefully. The rest of it was a blur. To be worked out, I decided.

What with the dawdling and the daydreaming I was late for breakfast but when I arrived I realized I wasn't the only late comer. My parents came from their bedroom yawning and half asleep. Jace, as usual, was bright and alert and already making coffee with the old coffee maker as the cappuccino machine stood in a corner, shiny and bright and somehow superior to everyone but me. If I didn't dust it regularly it wouldn't be shiny at all because I was the only one who knew how to use it and dust constantly settled in all the creases and crevices of the silver colored behemoth.

I looked for Russell but he hadn't come out of his room yet. "He's the one who was in a hurry to see that plant in the forest," I said to the room at large. "And he's still asleep."

"That's odd," my mother commented. "He's an early riser."

The words were barely out of my mother's mouth when Jace was away from the coffee maker and running towards Russell's bedroom. Moments later he returned, swearing under his breath. "He's gone."

My mother rolled her eyes. "Sounds like Russell. Doesn't believe in rules. Doesn't obey them when he should. Goes his own way. Does his own thing."

"He went to find the barberry bush."

My mother knew her co-worker. "Don't worry about him. He's used to the wilderness. Been in numerous ticklish situations. Think's he's immortal and is competent."

"And will get himself killed eventually if not today," Jace finished for her.

"He'll be fine." She'd worked with Russell for years and wasn't worried.

"I'm going after him." Jace grabbed a cup of coffee and downed it in one gulp, shaking his head at the hot liquid and muttering things to himself we couldn't hear. Probably for the best.

"I'll go with you." My mother rose.

He shook his head. "You stay here. No sense in exposing any more of us to possible danger than necessary."

My father began pacing. "Do you really think he

could be in danger?"

Jace shrugged. "Hopefully not. It's just a precaution."

"But you don't think that, do you?"

Jace made sure his Glock was strapped to his waist. "I never think one way or another. Take care of Brynn."

And he was out the door and striding towards the nearest path. I mentally followed him, knowing where he was going. The trail cam pointing towards the barberry bush was the farthest one from the cabin. If it was dangerous out there for Russell wasn't it just as much so for Jace?

We were waiting on the deck when he returned. He looked at us and said simply, "They got him. He's gone."

"How do you know?"

My mother was hopeful. "Maybe he's off the path and looking for more bushes."

Jace held out Russell's sat phone. "I found this." He turned it over. "It's still in its holder and the holder was snapped to his belt." He showed us how the leather holder had been cut. "It was discarded. It was in the brush. I only noticed it because it reflected a stray sunbeam. Without that unnatural shine in the only spot where the sun could get through the trees I'd never have noticed it."

"Whoever took him threw it away so it couldn't be traced."

Jace nodded grimly. "It's the only explanation."

We stood around numbly, breakfast forgotten. Everything was forgotten except Russell who was now the hostage we'd fought so hard to prevent.

I spoke up. "It should have been me. I'm the one they keep threatening to kidnap."

Jace touched my arm. Just touched it. "He was there and you weren't. Believe me, they'd rather have you but since they failed to get you they took whoever they could get and that turned out to be Russell."

My father stared at the tree-covered landscape. "Which means they've been watching all this time because the first and only time one person ventured out alone that person was grabbed."

It was ironic. Russell had traveled the world and been in many dangerous places and this place of rest and safety was where he'd been caught by thugs. The forest I'd known and loved all my life suddenly appeared menacing. Too green, too large, too secretive.

My father stared at Jace. "Can you track them?"

Jace shook his head. "I tried. There was a struggle, I could tell that much. Your friend put up a fight and as a result the entire area is so disturbed that it's impossible to separate any one track from another. Maybe a seasoned wilderness tracker could figure it out but not me."

"Then what can we do?" My mother was close to tears. She and Russell had worked side by side for years. Their relationship was close, mentor and mentee, one generation and another.

Jace stood for a long time, thinking. "We can't just go out and start looking. The forest is too big and if we go we could also get grabbed. So the only solution is to find out who took him. Then we go after whoever that is and threaten them until they tell us where he is and hope he's still okay when we get there."

"How do we do that?" My father rocked back on his heels as he regarded Jace. "We don't know who's after the formula so we don' t know who took him. That's been the biggest problem from day one."

"I'll call John Wilder. Maybe he's learned something." His gaze took in the entire forest that spread out for miles in every direction. "If he knows nothing yet then maybe we comb the woods one cabin at a time. But I hope it doesn't come to that."

Russell was an old man. How much time did we have before his elderly body gave out? My mother bit her lower lip to hold back tears and I wished I could cry for her. "That'll take forever."

"Yes it will if it comes to that. If we can't identify the kidnappers." Jace agreed somberly. "So let's hope John knows something."

John Wilder Investigations didn't know where Russell could be held but they had learned that Henry Torelle was even more corrupt than anyone had thought. Henry knew which company had threatened my family and didn't care. In fact he was negotiating with them along with two other companies to manufacture the immunity drug and planned to go with whichever would pay the most, the only important fee being the one for him. Plus his finder's fee.

The phone was on speaker so we heard both sides of Jace's conversation with his friend.

"I'll lean on him." Said by John Wilder.

"How can that help find Russell?" Jace wanted to know.

"I don't yet know but maybe I'll get a brilliant idea while bashing his head in." Said by John Wilder in a pleasant voice as if discussing the warmth of a summer's day.

"Get to it ASAP because Russell is tough as nails for someone his age but he's reached an age where he can crash at any time."

"Will do."

The call ended and my father began pacing. Of course he did. This time, though, Jace joined him and my mother and I watched in amazement as the two men pretended to check security around the cabin – and then check it again – and then again -- while in reality they were venting energy they'd prefer using on whoever had Russell.

When John Wilder called back they raced each other to the phone. John was hopeful. "Your friend doesn't want to go to jail so he's agreed to cooperate in exchange for me not telling the authorities what I recently found out about him and some of his business dealings." John's voice said what he thought of Henry Torelle.

"How does that help us?"

"He's agreed to talk to the company that's threatening you guys. Has to be the ones who took Russell. He'll say he needs to know where Russell is and that he must be safe and returned ASAP in order for him to continue negotiations with them.

"He'll say he doesn't care personally what happens to Russell – and that'll be the truth so it'll sound right to whoever he's talking to – but he'll insist the deal must include Russell's quick release."

"Sounds good. When will it happen?"

"We are placing a wire on him as we speak."

"Will he be safe? Is it dangerous?"

"Not as dangerous as the alternative because we are very persuasive." There was a pause, then, "Besides, he made the choice all by himself. After we had a little chat about the law and what prisons are like and a few other interesting topics."

"Is this ethical?"

"It's totally ethical for an upstanding citizen to help implicate a nefarious company." John's laughter was clear over the phone and put smiles on our faces even as we worried about Russell.

When the phone call ended the pacing resumed. The waiting. My father and Jace. Back and forth, Jace's hands behind his backs, my father's crutches thumping, both with heads down.

My mother and I simply watched and drank endless cups of coffee. Cappuccino, actually, as I made good use of the shiny machine in the kitchen but it wasn't enough to make me forget how slow the clock hands moved as we waited for another phone call.

It was better than wearing a hole in the floor like the guys were doing and when I presented my father and Jace with foamy mugs of cappuccino they stopped pacing long enough to slosh down the drinks.

Then Jace's phone rang. He answered as we all held our breaths. He listened. His eyes slitted. He licked his lips and his gaze met mine saying the news wouldn't be good. I blinked my response, that we'd deal with whatever he was about to say. Somehow.

He clicked his phone off. "They called an ambulance." We went even more silent than before. "For Henry Torelle. The visit with the pharmaceutical company didn't go well. The wire was discovered. He was dumped, beaten and unconscious in an alley with no way to know who brought him there or where they came from because the wire was gone."

"Poor Henry."

"He knew the risk and it was the kind of thing that was inevitable, given his lifestyle."

"Will he live?"

"Too early to tell. They hope so."

"The whole plan was for nothing." My father pounded one fist into the other. "And we still don't know where Russell was taken."

Jace looked at me again, grimly, then at my father. "So we figure things out a different way."

"How?" My mother's expression was devoid of hope.

I stepped between Jace and my father and spoke because Jace was right and my mind was suddenly working overtime. "There's always another way." Jace looked lost but my plan was formulating as I spoke. "Surely we can do here the same thing here that John Wilder is doing in the city."

"Like what?"

CHAPTER 20

After long minutes of thought on all our parts I told them my still forming idea. "Russell was kidnapped nearby so it makes sense they took him somewhere nearby. To their base camp. I'm sure they have one because they'd need a place to take me if they could get me. The forest makes it easy to have one without being noticed."

"It's a huge area. Where do we start? And how?"

I looked at the computer monitor with the trail cam footage. But it wasn't the only computer in the cabin. We kept several for company or for our own use. "Most detective work is done using computers. Isn't it? And we have lots of them."

Jace gave me a look that said I was right. "So how can we find potential places thugs might choose for a base of operations?" He raked his fingers through that short hair. "Henry would have been taken there in lieu of you."

I worked with computers all the time. Yes, I

worked with numbers but the concept was the same. Look up a few things and find the proper information.

My father was ahead of me. "We'll find him using the high-speed internet that costs a fortune because we're in the boonies." His brows knit in determination. He turned towards me. "Brynn, you use computers all the time at your job." Just what I'd been thinking. "Can you do it?"

We moved towards the office where the computer monitor showed the trail cams. I pulled a second laptop from a shelf and booted it up and then turned to everyone. Me because I'm the nerd in the family. Not an expert but better than anyone else in the room. "What do we need to know?"

Jace raked his hair again in thought. "You know about the cabins in the area. Who owns them, who lives here year-around and who's just here in the summer." He frowned in remembrance of that day on the hilltop overlooking the forest. "You said most are family owned. The kidnappers wouldn't have chosen any of them even if they are empty because the owners might show up at the wrong time."

"They have weapons. They could disarm the owners."

"No reason to do something so drastic if there are cabins they can occupy legitimately without calling attention to themselves."

I saw where he was going. "And because this is a vacation area at any given time cabins will be available for rent. So we find out which ones are now being rented."

"You pointed out one such. Renting it would provide a legitimate reason for them to be in the area and there must be at least a couple near enough to your cabin to accomplish their ends." Our looks met. "So that rental cabin you first pointed out is where we start. Can you find out if it's been rented recently or, more importantly, has renters in it now?"

Finding the answer took a while. None of us knew what company owned the cabin I'd pointed out to Jace and the Chamber of Commerce wasn't helpful until we said we were looking for a place to rent for a rather large family reunion and that money was no object.

Then they insisted on naming every resort in the area large enough to hold a lot of people along with a very long list of amenities for each. We had to listen to the entire list for each resort after which we politely informed them that resort wouldn't meet our needs. Eventually they realized that none of the resorts on their list would work for us which was good because by then we were running out of reasons why we needed to learn about other places for rent.

They finally suggested the Mallory Company cabin as a last, desperate possibility. "They rent it out when the company isn't using it." I sagged in weariness because at last we were getting somewhere. "It might work for a family reunion."

We had it. The name of the company and. wonder

of wonders, we were given the company phone number.

I yelled like a cheerleader when the Mallory secretary answered and politely and generically asked how she could help. The poor woman would have hung up in shock when she heard me scream in joy but for what must have been extensive training in how to deal with idiots on the phone.

My enthusiasm didn't last long. "You want to rent the cabin?" A pause was followed by what might have been real regret. "Sorry, but it's full now and will be for the foreseeable future."

I thought fast. "I was told it was empty but that was a couple weeks ago. Maybe it was empty then and was rented so it's full now?"

A pause as the secretary checked something. "I can't imagine who told you that. It's been in constant use by Mallory all summer. Meetings, vacations, that sort of thing."

"Oh." What else was there to say? "Guess I was mistaken."

The secretary politely hoped we'd find a place for our family reunion and then hung up as quickly as good manners allowed.

My mother said what we were thinking. "It wasn't the Mallory cabin. So now what do we do?"

I thought back to that day Jace and I had studied the forest. "There's one other possibility."

Jace knew what I was thinking. "The cabin that's for sale." He added, "It's empty so no one is likely to come upon them unexpectedly. It's their best bet since the Mallory cabin is occupied."

"It's probably locked."

"Locks can be broken."

"We should check it out."

We stared longer. "Who should go?"

My father examined each of us in turn. "Jace is the only one with the necessary skills for something like this but guarding Brynn is his job and she should stay here so he should too."

I stood as tall as possible. "Jace can go. I'll be fine here. We have rifles. Several of different calibers and sizes."

"What if Jace is caught?" My father scowled. "I'm sure there are several kidnappers. Maybe many. If that happens they can come for Brynn."

Jace headed for the land line phone. "I'll call John. They do protection as well as investigations. He'll send someone."

"It'll take the better part of a day for that someone to get here. We can't wait."

Jace scowled. "I can't leave you guys alone."

"Yes you can," my father said, switching from his previous insistence that Jace had to stay with me. Possibly because of my mother's expression. She was mentally seeing Russell, the elderly man who surely couldn't handle much more. "We'll be fine while you go get Russell."

I saw things differently. "If these people are as

efficient as they've been so far then one man can't rescue Russell by himself."

"I won't try. I'll just monitor the situation and wait for reinforcements."

"That'll be at least a day. Probably two."

"Russell is old and fragile." My mother's voice showed the depth of her concern and her face grew grayer and older with each passing minute. "I don't know how long he can hold out, especially if they aren't treating him well and they don't care what happens to him. He's expendable. Even if we give them the formula they might only return his body."

"We must all go." I stepped to Jace and touched him briefly. Our looks met and I felt his emotion as it poured from him and into me. I was stunned by it. Knocked sidewise by the feelings in that look. Warmed by it. "Except my father stays behind because he's on crutches."

I met Jace's look full on until he, too, felt something going directly from me to him. His expression didn't change but the color of his eyes did. They deepened. Darkened. Turned into bottomless pools. He didn't want me in danger but someone had to find Russell.

I took a deep breath and said what I was thinking. "We have rifles, both my mother and know how to use them and three people are better than one."

"I don't like that idea." Jace and my father both spoke at the same time. Jace's eyes were stormy with indecision.

"I know the forest. You don't, not really. I know it better than anyone else in this room."

My mother folded over at her waist. "I've been all over the world. I know how to take care of myself and I don't see any other option. If we wait for John Wilder's people to get here we could be too late. I don't think Russell can last that long."

She sighed. "It's been coming for a while. I've talked to him about his age and that he should slow down but he insists he's just as spry as when he was young." She shook her head sadly. "He's not."

One look at my mother's face said she wouldn't wait for John Wilder's men. Jace gave me another long look and then reluctantly agreed to my plan. He examined my mother trying to decide if she'd been telling the truth when she said she'd be helpful. I nodded imperceptibly that, yes, she knew how to deal with a lot of situations. "Okay. We three go. But make sure you are armed and promise to do exactly what I say, when I say and don't ask questions because that'll slow things down."

We agreed though it was easy to see my father didn't like the idea of staying back. But he had no choice. Soon we set out at a steady pace along the trail nearest to the cabin with me leading and rifles strapped to our backs. When the trail branched we turned left and found ourselves picking up speed as we neared our destination.

It was a perfect summer day. No clouds in the sky, no wind to speak of. The lack of wind was bad because everything was still so the sound buffer of the undergrowth was less than usual.

After a few minutes of walking Jace indicated with his hand that we should slow down and move quietly. We did so and that slowed our progress quite a bit but eventually the small, old log cabin with a 'for sale' sign in the yard came into view.

Jace nodded. We soon saw why. The cabin was occupied. We huddled to hear what he had to say because he spoke softly. "It isn't necessarily the kidnappers. This could be totally innocent. Vacationers. People who wandered by and saw the 'for sale' sign and decided to check it out." He waved a hand. "There are a dozen reasons this might not be what we think it is."

My mother was grim. "Or it might be exactly what it looks like and Russell is in there."

Jace looked us over. Two people with deadly weapons who didn't know a thing about warfare and one who did. Jace. He sighed, then spoke. "You guys stay here. Don't follow me."

He continued. "Keep your rifles at the ready and be alert but don't do anything unless I tell you to." We nodded but he still didn't start towards the log cabin. Didn't do anything except stare at us. Now that our goal was in sight, he clearly wished he was alone and we were somewhere else. "I mean it. Nothing at all unless you hear me shout."

He added, "I'll yell so loud they'll hear me in town so don't worry about missing my signal." He ended his short speech with another heartfelt sigh. "In other words don't do anything stupid. Please."

We watched him quietly and carefully make his way to the back of the cabin, rifle in hand and at the ready. He checked the area from the green curtain of the forest and then looked through the windows from a distance to avoid being seen if someone was inside and chanced to look out.

Confident of what he saw from that distance so he needn't worry about being seen he crossed the small open space to the cabin and sidled along the wall until he reached the closest window and peered inside.

He glanced around the room quickly and then moved to one side so as not to be seen by anyone in the cabin. He turned towards us, nodded, and gave the thumbs-up sign. It was all we could do not to erupt in cheers. My mother's whisper said it all. "He's there. Russell is in the cabin and Jace will get him free."

There was no doubt in her mind. None in either of our minds. He could do it though I wondered how he'd accomplish the impossible. I realized how many possibilities there were for things to go wrong. For Russell to suffer. For Jace to die. My stomach clenched and I had to bend over to keep from being sick.

That was when I realized I was in love with Jace. It couldn't have happened at the worst possible time.

Truly in love, not just heading in that direction. Not just thinking about it. There was no maybe about it. I was in love with Jace. Totally. Completely. And if things didn't go right I could lose him before I even had him.

But there was a job to be done so I bit my lip and did my best to shove emotion aside and be ready. I failed completely and hoped against hope that I wouldn't ruin everything.

We watched as Jace carefully pried the window loose from its frame and beckoned for Russell to climb out, supporting him as he shimmied through and dropped to the ground. As they turned to come towards us we held our breaths. Tightened our grips on our rifles. Hoped we'd not have to use them.

Then the worst thing possible happened.

A man came around the corner of the cabin. Saw Jace and Russell. Stopped for a mini-second in shock. Then shouted. Yelled. Screamed. "He's out! The old man is free!"

Jace grabbed Russell and dragged the elderly man towards the trees. They reached comparative safety as three other men came running. The newcomers carried rifles but by then Jace and Russell were behind a huge tree. Without a target the kidnappers couldn't shoot so they ran towards them.

Jace fired two shots. He didn't hit anyone which meant he hadn't intended to as he dragged Russell deeper into the forest.

We didn't know what to do. If we shot would we

hit the kidnappers or Jace and Russell?

I made a decision. I wouldn't hit them if I was at a different angle. I might not hit anyone, in fact, but if I shot in the general direction of the kidnappers it might slow them down. So I threw brush aside and ran away and to one side, crashing through brush as I went. As soon as I got close enough I'd start shooting.

But I stumbled. Crashed around trying to regain my footing. And found myself being grabbed on both sides as a guttural voice in my ear said. "Got you!"

CHAPTER 21

Another voice said, "Forget the man. We have the girl. Let's get out of here." And I felt myself being dragged.

I fought with every bit of strength I had. I kicked. I hit. I twisted. I screamed. Then I screamed louder. Nothing did any good. Nothing stopped them. As their grip on me grew stronger I was dragged faster and even faster through the woods. And still I screamed until a rag was stuffed in my mouth and then there was nothing I could do.

But the trail we were making must be obvious. I fought harder in order to leave a clear trail, knowing my kidnappers didn't have the time to cover their tracks. Jace would see my trail. He would come.

Then, abruptly, the dragging stopped. I couldn't speak but I could see. We'd reached a tiny creek, one of many in the area and my captors followed it upstream, dragging me through the cold water, leaving no trace of our movements, making no sound to betray our presence.

Walking in the creek left no trail and Jace couldn't follow a trail that didn't exist.

Not far upstream they left the creek and dragged me to a small shed that looked like it had been constructed hastily but with enough brush covering it that it would be hard to find if you didn't know it was there.

Where were we? I knew the forest but had been too busy fighting my captors to pay attention. Were we close to the cabin? Had Russell been taken here when he was first captured and held here until the coast was clear to take him to the cabin?

They threw me inside and a board was slammed across the door. The shack was small and crudely built with odd sized boards thrown together haphazardly before being screwed together. Because of those screws there was no way they could be taken apart but it had been so quickly built that I could see outside easily through cracks and even through the brush that concealed it.

I heard my captors slump to the ground and cover themselves with detritus from the forest floor, making themselves a part of the brush pushed against the sides of the shed. They might be thugs but they'd known how to bring me there without being followed and they knew how things looked in the forest. We were invisible.

Moments later I heard their whispered voices on a cell phone telling someone they had me. That they had the upper hand and everything was good. Their voices were triumphant.

"We want our money." They were not only triumphant, they were greedy. "This job was more than you said. We want a bonus and we want it now and then we want to be gone."

The conversation ended and they checked on me. They were almost friendly. Almost. "This is just business, you know." They looked me over, a tall man with a beard and another, almost bald, a bit shorter but with bulging muscles. "We turn you over and then we'll be out of your hair."

They indicated that if I screamed they'd keep the rag in my mouth but if I promised to be quiet they'd take it out. I nodded that I understood and soon I could speak. "What'll happen to me?" They shrugged that they didn't know. "Will I be hurt?" Killed? Worse?

"You'll find out soon enough," the bald one said, not wishing me to be hurt but not caring enough to prevent it. "After you rest a bit and we make sure we weren't followed we'll leave."

"Where will you take me?

Another shrug. "That's not our concern. We turn you over, we get paid, and we go as far as we can from that crazy man with a rifle who sticks to you like a burr." They laughed. "It was lucky for us he broke that old guy free because that's the only time he's left your side since we've been watching you."

"You do know what this is all about, don't you?" What could I say to make them change their plans? "That it's not about me? It's about money."

Another shrug. "It's always about money."

"Whatever you're being paid, it's not enough."

That got their attention. "Why not?"

"We're talking billions of dollars for the people who want me. Billions." I let that sink in, hoping they'd take the bait. "How much are they paying you? I bet not much."

They merely looked at each other and laughed. The bearded one said, "Good try, kid."

I sank against the wall of the tiny shed ignoring what must be a thousand crawling insects attracted by the brush that concealed it. I closed my eyes and tried to rest. My legs burned and I was covered with cuts from the brush I'd been dragged through.

I tried to think what to do next. How to free myself before they turned me over to whoever had paid them to kidnap me because when that person got me I didn't know if I'd live or die. Most likely, die.

Then I heard it. A sound so subtle that it blended with the usual forest noises. If I wasn't so attuned to Jace I'd not have heard it. But the sound I heard was Jace. I knew it was him because he had a way of moving in the forest or the jungle or any uneven terrain that was different from anyone I'd known. A military thing? Was he trained to move that way? Or was I simply so tuned to him that I knew him separate from everyone else on Earth? I didn't know how I knew. All I knew was that Jace Browne was nearby.

I opened my eyes and checked the forest through the cracks in the shed walls but saw nothing. No Jace. No movement beyond the usual shivering of the leaves on the bushes around the shed that turned what little sunlight got through the overhead canopy into flashes of silver and green.

Except there was no wind, hadn't been any so we'd had to go slowly in order not to make any sound when we headed to the cabin. There definitely wasn't enough wind to move any leaves this close to the ground where even the tiniest of breezes would be totally extinguished. And yet now, in that silence, the leaves moved.

It was Jace and he was there.

A hand appeared beside the wall of the shed inches from me that was soon replaced by Jace's face, concern all over it and something I couldn't read. Regret? Apology? Something else?

The slits in the wall were only enough to fit a finger through but I did what I could and we touched. Not a word was spoken but that light touch said it all. He'd take care of things.

He indicated I lay flat and I did so. Then he disappeared and the weak sunlight once more came through the slits as he disappeared. I tried to follow his progress around the shed but the movement I'd seen when he came had been the only movement in the sparse sunlight. Now he was in shade and totally invisible.

Then I heard nothing. Until I heard a grunt followed by more silence. After a few moments I heard another grunt and that was all. No shots. No screams. Nothing to tell me what was happening.

I waited, not knowing I was holding my breath until the door of the shed was pushed open and Jace appeared, a smile a mile wide on his face and I knew everything was going to be okay.

He hauled me upright and we exited the shed.

"I need to get these guys stable now." He grabbed rope from somewhere on his person and soon the two thugs were trussed up like a couple of pigs on their way to market. Then Jace turned to me. Examined me and his expression said what he'd gone through since learning I'd been taken.

He had to clear his throat before he could speak. Even then his voice was hoarse. "I was terrified. I was afraid I wouldn't get to you in time." Not terrified that he wouldn't find me because that was never in doubt, just that it might take longer than it should. "I failed you."

I laughed. Not out of humor, exactly, but because of what he'd just said. "Failed me? Are you kidding!? You saved Russell and you saved me and you caught the bad guys." My words were met with his wan smile.

Then he changed. Took a deep breath. Looked around at the forest that was still there and as immense and unknowable as ever. Then he kind of shook his head. Then he grinned. Then he reached for me and soon we were as close as physically possible considering we were wearing camo designed to shed brush and twigs without being punctured or torn. But even through all those layers I could feel his heart beating. I could see his breath going in and out. I could read those expressive eyes and know I was safe and would be safe forever.

My mother showed up a long time after that. The thugs were awake by then and seething with silent anger. We all made our way to the cabin where my father waited with eyes drawn with terror because he hadn't known what was happening. Jace called John Wilder and asked what to do next.

John Wilder's men showed up in what seemed like minutes and was probably longer. John himself would be along as soon as possible, they said. He was still in New York and wanted to contact a few people and get a few things straightened out before coming.

John's men took the thugs into custody. My parents, Russell, Jace, and I dropped onto whatever chair or couch was handy and stared blankly at one another until I made drinks for us in that cappuccino machine that no one else knew how to operate.

The simple act made my parents smile. Their smiles were lopsided and small but were the beginning of a return to normal and when the drinks were ready and distributed so everyone had a hot, foamy cappuccino I sank onto the couch and curled up next to Jace because I had to be close to him. Had to be.

He said nothing but put an arm around me in a way that was not only protective but also possessive and I gloried in it. It was also a very public declaration of the fact that we were together. The action made my father smile and his eyes gleam. Jace and I took in that gleam and looked at one another.

Then Jace started a slow grin that became a smile that spread all across his face as he pulled me even closer before turning to my father and saying, "You're going to get what you wanted, Mr. Peters."

My father's expression was so fatuous that my mother and Russell looked at him in alarm. Then my father spoke up. "Are you saying I'm about to get a son-in-law?"

"I hope so." Jace turned me towards him and asked with his eyes if he could be my father's son-in-law. My husband. "I think so," he said next with just the tiniest bit of uncertainty until my answering snort said of course that was how things would be and how could he have any doubts that I would gladly and happily spend the rest of my life with him.

Then, right there in front of everyone, Jace kissed me. Hard. My father cheered loudly and my mother and Russell had to be brought up to date on all that had happened romance-wise while they'd been away discovering the newest and most potent immunology drug yet.

My mother glowered at my father's underhanded way of getting the son-in-law he wanted. But she didn't glower long because she knew he'd never change. And because she liked Jace.

It had been a tumultuous day. We were all exhausted. When the cappuccinos were done and I'd heated up some left-over roast and veggies that we ate sitting anywhere comfortable because we were too weary to gather around a table for a formal meal we went to bed and slept the night away and half the next morning. Jace slept in the room next to me because he no longer needed to be close. Darn it, anyway.

John Wilder showed up the next afternoon.

"Those guys are in jail and can't stop talking because giving up their bosses will mean lighter sentences for them."

"Do they know what pharmaceutical company was behind everything?"

"They don't but it's just a matter of time before we trace the order for Brynn's kidnapping back to its originator. There are enough greedy pharmaceuticals out there that it could be any of several." He paused, then continued. "Hopefully when this is done it'll send a message through the pharmaceutical industry. It'll say 'don't be stupid.'"

"Think it'll make a difference?"

John's expression said he doubted it. "Maybe for a while and that's better than not at all and sometimes we have to be content with the wars we win knowing there will be more in the future. But that's okay. We'll win those too. Eventually." His voice was confident. The man was another Jace.

EPILOGUE

We were married in the cabin, in front of the huge split-rock fireplace. Of course we were. No place else would have been right. It was a small, intimate ceremony with only John Wilder and Russell there in addition to my parents. There was a pastor, of course, who kept an eye on the weather because he was local and our driveway was infamous in the area and he didn't want to be stuck there for days if it rained. Or longer.

My father kept an eye on the weather for the same reason except he was hoping for storms because if everyone was stranded he'd get to play host in his very favorite place in the whole world.

Jase and I hoped for good weather so we wouldn't have to spend our honeymoon in the company of other people because if it was pouring out we'd not want to sleep in a tent. We'd have to stay in the huge log cabin that would allow for plenty of privacy that still wouldn't be enough for us.

We got the beautiful weather we wanted and were able to disappear into that forest with the camping equipment that would be our home while we got used to being married. We didn't say when we'd return because we didn't know. "You'll see us again when we show up."

My mother worried. "What if something happens to you? You'll be out there in the wilderness."

My father snorted and told her she shouldn't be judging us after her galivanting through some of the most inhospitable places on earth in search of new drugs. She turned kind of red and wished us a happy honeymoon.

We didn't need her good wishes but they were nice. As soon as the pastor left along the driveway with thanks that he could get to the road safely we shouldered our packs and headed for the forest. And each other.

THE END

Hi,

I hope you enjoyed *Guarding Brynn*.

If you want to see what else I've written, check out my website at http://www.FlorenceWitkop.com
If you'd like to leave a review of *Guarding Brynn*, click on the link beneath the *Guarding Brynn* cover and you'll be directed to the Amazon page where reviews can be posted.

***

My next book is *Come To Me*. It's a contemporary, clean and wholesome romance with a healthy dose of action and adventure and a sci-fi/paranormal twist that make for a good page-turning read. Here's the back cover info that tells what it's about:

Two strangers. One direction. North. Just go north.

Jude Fielding and Diedre Brown can neither resist nor ignore a sudden, overwhelming compulsion to go north. No questions. No answers. Just get in Jude's SUV and head north.

As they drive, a mysterious entity enters their minds and speaks to them. It says it chose them with care. It insists they are perfect for its purpose. That they compliment each other precisely. And that their love will remain steadfast as they carry out its projects.

But they aren't in love. At least they don't think they are. And there's no way they'll trust a voice in their heads.

Then the entity reveals one more thing. Their journey north is merely the first stage of a new, amazing, and totally unique life it has planned for them, one filled with adventure and a deep and lasting love.

Something is waiting for them just a bit farther north. It could be wonderful. Or the embodiment of evil.

Dare they find out which?

Now that you know a little of what *Come To Me* is about, here's the beginning. It'll be published by Winged Publications in the not too distant future, will be available on Amazon, and will be free with Kindle Unlimited.

COME TO ME

by

Florence Witkop

PROLOGUE

The road ahead was dark. Too dark. Jude gripped the steering wheel and tried to see enough to keep going but the rain poured down the outside of the windows like a waterfall. The windshield wipers couldn't keep up. We couldn't continue. It would be suicide.

The road curved. Jude slowed but the rain-slicked highway didn't allow for much control so we slid around the curve, gradually slowing to half speed. When it seemed we'd made it safely a truck appeared from the opposite direction.

The truck loomed closer and closer. Then the worst thing possible happened as it reached the curve. It hit a slick spot, went out of control, slid sidewise and headed across the center line towards us.

It was a large truck, a semi that would turn Jude's SUV into little pieces and us along with it. We were about to be broadsided because not even Jude, the consummate jet pilot, could avoid a collision, not in the rain, not on pavement that resembled black ice more than concrete.

Then, at the last second Jude accelerated. He powered the SUV until it flew through the night as he pointed it towards the side of the road to avoid the inevitable collision. We swerved wildly enough that if there'd been another vehicle on the road or if he hadn't got us past that semi there'd have been a major accident.

But he managed.

When the wild swings subsided, he pulled to the side of the road, put on the emergency blinkers, and dropped his head to the steering wheel as the semi passed us and continued down the road. Then he lifted his head and looked through the windshield, staring into the dark and the rain.

"We can't continue."

"Will it let us stop? The compulsion? Will it?"

Jude considered the road ahead. "We need sleep. Everyone does. Surely whoever – whatever -- is doing this to us will let us rest."

We looked at each other.

Could we stop? We didn't know.

If so, where could we spend the night? We didn't know.

Were there motels in the area? We didn't know.

Was there a town ahead? We didn't know that either.

What did we know? Very little.

We didn't know why we were driving through the night in a storm of epic proportions with rain sluicing along the car.

We didn't know why we couldn't stop.

We didn't know why we were in such a panic to drive north. No other direction. Just north.

We didn't know our destination.

Or how long it would take to reach it.

Or what we'd find when we got there.

Neither of us knew.

We just knew we *had* to do it. *Had* to keep going. *Had* to keep heading north. *Had* to get somewhere. *Had* to.

We had no choice in the matter. None at all.

CHAPTER 1

Days earlier – actually a week or so earlier, though time became confusing after a while -- an elderly man had held a door open for me.

I was charmed as he smiled and tipped his head. I couldn't know what was behind the thoughtful, old-world gesture, but I loved it. It made me feel special. As I passed, he raised his head slightly to meet my look and smiled even more in an enigmatic way. As if he knew something I didn't and I found that, too, to be charming.

Then he moved towards parts unknown, and I entered the building and went in search of my first seminar. I expected to forget all about him in seconds.

I didn't. All during that seminar I mentally blocked out the speaker and instead saw the elderly man. The silver hair that was thick and shiny in a rather long cut. The sparkle in his faded blue eyes. The courtly gestures that had been so unexpected and had made me feel special. And that enigmatic something about him.

I found myself smiling internally while trying to remember to take notes on the finer points of raising puppies that would later become service dogs. Because that's what the convention was about. It was why so many people had converged on the huge building with the large, heavy, carved doors that he'd held open. Service dogs. It was why I was there.

Other than the somewhat unusual topic of service dogs, though, the convention was like all conventions.

Loud and chaotic. Soon after leaving that first seminar, I developed a headache. It appeared full blown as I made my way through the crowded, noisy halls to my next event. I tried to make headway and failed completely.

I pulled the map of the building from my purse and tried to figure where I should be next, checking the map while walking and wishing my head would stop throbbing. Bad move on my part because I walked straight into a solid object. No, I realized, as I studied the object before me. Not an object at all. A person. A man.

Oops.

I turned red and backed up a couple feet and was about to turn away and disappear in the crowd when my victim reached out and grabbed my hand. I froze but he held me lightly. Nothing nasty even though I'd almost run him over, though judging from the solid bulk before me, it would have taken a lot more than me to knock him off his feet. Two of me, at least. Or three.

"Are you okay?" *He* was worried about *me*? I ran into him, not the other way around. But he chose tact and said, "We had a collision."

I nodded while avoiding eye contact. I was that embarrassed. But even through my eyelashes I could tell he was tallish, well built and didn't seem angry. The not angry part was the important thing. I cautiously raised my head until I could see him straight-on. "I'm sorry. It was my fault."

"No, it wasn't. I bumped into you." He looked around and kind of hauled me out of the flow of traffic because if we stayed where we were we'd both be knocked sidewise. "Or maybe we were pushed into each other by this veritable sea of humanity." A sudden grin split his face. "Though if either of us had become unbalanced, we'd not have fallen because it's too crowded to allow for a decent fall."

Not only was he tallish and well built, he had a sense of humor and was nice. Decent. Trying to make me feel better and since he seemed to be waiting for me to say something, I said the first thing that came into my mind and that was about service dogs because it was a convention for people who dealt with them. "Do you train service dogs?"

He shook his head as a woman in a hurry knocked me towards the wall on her way to somewhere but he grabbed me before I hit. His reaction time was amazing, his arms strong. "Nope."

"Then are you with someone who's looking for one?"

"Nope again."

The crowd thinned as people got to wherever they were headed for their next seminar. But it was still busy and the hum of talk made it necessary to step close to be heard. "But surely you have something to do with service dogs or you'd not be here." I was becoming curious.

"I do not deal with them, nor do I know anything about them." He expertly diverted a couple who almost plowed into us as he kind of hovered over me protectively. I was grateful. "But the people I work for do know a lot and they are big donors. They were invited. So here I am."

"Oh. You're here on business."

"Yes, but I have nothing to do until they are ready to leave and that'll be when the convention ends. Three days. So I decided to look around and see what the whole thing is about." He checked both ways along the hall and when he saw the coast was clear he moved away from the wall, and I followed.

"There seems to be a lot to learn but in all honesty I'm ready for a break even though it's still early morning. I'm dying for a cup of coffee." His eyebrows quirked in a question. "Want to join me and we can compare war stories? If you don't have someplace to be."

"I'm signed up for another seminar. But I'm not sure I'll go. I have a headache." Which was getting worse by the second.

He looked around the hall that was semi-empty by then. "You are already late. Everyone will look at you when you enter the room and that'll make your headache worse." He grinned like a kid playing hooky. "I have nothing to do, and the day is just starting. What say you come with me, and I'll treat you to coffee and aspirin. I have some with me."

I didn't have aspirin and he did, and I wanted some. So I looked along the corridor and momentarily closed my eyes against the headache and said, "Sure. Let's go."

An hour later the headache was less, and I knew his name was Jude Fielding and he was a corporate jet pilot who'd flown in a bevy of business types who were considering giving a considerable amount of money to help raise and train service dogs.

In that time over coffee, he'd also learned a lot about me. "You are Diedre Brown, and you raise and socialize puppies in your spare time until they are ready to attend doggie school." He tipped his head exactly as the elderly man had done earlier and I wondered whether the gesture this time was courtesy or curiosity. Either way, I liked it. "And where did you stash your current puppy so you could attend the convention?"

"I'm between puppies at the moment."

I looked beyond him and was surprised to see the elderly man with the silver hair enter the coffee bar. The man who'd held the door for me earlier. Our eyes met and he nodded and smiled, and I couldn't help doing the same. Jude turned around to see who I was smiling at. "You know him?"

I told him what had happened. "And he remembers you and you remember him after just a few seconds at the entrance?" He examined the elderly man. "Though now I see him, I think I might have talked with him earlier. Just like you. At the door, right?" I nodded as the elderly man turned his smile towards Jude. It was both polite and genuine. "Yes, he's the man I saw. I remember now, just like you remembered. That smile is impossible to forget."

"He seemed nice."

Jude agreed that he was nice as he and the elderly man nodded to each other. Then Jude turned back to me and the elderly man ordered a coffee that he took somewhere else while Jude and I refilled ours and took them outside and sat on the steps of the convention building because it was the lovely kind of day that promised to make the rest of my headache disappear. And it did.

When our coffee was gone, we didn't go our separate ways. Instead, we spent the rest of that day together. Not for any reason and not because of some sudden inner connection. Rather I'd decided I didn't want to risk another headache and neither of us had anything special to do so we decided to do nothing together and the rest of that day turned out to be as lovely as our time sitting on the steps had been.

I decided Jude Fielding might be former military. He had the erect posture, short haircut and general air of competence that speaks of military service. He was also gorgeous in a tall-dark-and-handsome kind of way, and I enjoyed the looks from other women who thought Jude and I were actually an item. It was fun and laughable, relaxing and bubbly.

The day passed quickly. All too soon it was time to return to my motel and for Jude to go wherever he went while waiting to fly the corporate types back to wherever they came from. As we exited the building and separated, we looked back and saw the silver-haired man again. He waved at us with that memorable smile, and we waved back because he was a nice man and because we both felt like waving and smiling, and the elderly man gave us a good excuse to do so.

In my motel room I downloaded some work for a client who needed his books done immediately. Bookkeeping is like that and when you are self-employed it happens oftener than would seem possible. But I finished eventually and fell asleep quickly and easily and awoke the next morning ready for the second day of the convention. The day when I'd actually attend the seminars I'd signed up for.

CHAPTER 2

I didn't attend any seminars the next morning, either, and I didn't even feel guilty because spending the day with a man completely charming and friendly and interesting was much better than listening to someone drone on about how to raise the puppies I'd been raising long enough that I could probably teach him a few things.

That man wasn't Jude Fielding. He was the man I'd met at the entrance the first day of the convention and that second day happened almost exactly the same as the first, with a courteous nod of his head while he swept the door open for me. But this time I stopped and smiled broadly and was rewarded by a similar smile as he waved me through.

I don't know why I spoke. Perhaps because Jude and I had talked about him the previous day. Perhaps because his old-world courtesies had got to me. How many men treat women like that now? "Thank you."

He nodded. "You're welcome, lovely lady."

I blushed. Yes, I actually blushed. "Do you open the door for everyone?" Perhaps it was his job?

He shook his head. "Only for the truly nice people." His words were followed by a deprecating chuckle. "Which is almost everyone so perhaps it's as you suggest."

The door remained open, but I hesitated. "Are you some kind of gallant knight?"

He let the door close by itself as he straightened, eyes gleaming with intelligence and the kind of sunshine that had sent my headache away the previous day. "I can't pretend to be noble but good manners are never out of style."

"And you have them in abundance." I'd been curious about Jude the day before. I was curious now about this elderly silver-haired man. "Do you train service dogs?" If he did, he must be one of the best, the kind whose dogs were always polite and courteous and caring.

"No. I can't pretend to be as gifted as those who do. But I am impressed with everyone here." He cocked his head exactly as I remembered him doing before. "This place is full of people who love and care for living beings of a different species." He paused and his eyes shone with passion. "Such people are special. That's why I'm here. I find such people intriguing and I want to be around them for a brief moment." What he said next sealed my fate for the entirety of that morning. "People like you, Diedre Brown."

"You know my name." A statement not a question.

"You impressed me yesterday. I asked around." His eyebrows furrowed in a question." I hope you don't mind."

"Of course, I don't mind." He could be an axe murderer with a killer smile for all I knew but I returned that smile with one of my own. "And what's your name if you don't mind telling me?"

"Lourdes Jones at your service." He swept low in a bow and the two of us entered the building together as meetings, seminars and classes flew out of my mind because being with Lourdes Jones would be far, far more entertaining and when the convention ended, I'd have a special memory to take home with me. No doubt about it. He was that charismatic.

As it turned out, I only spent the morning with him. During that time, though, as we wandered the halls and took in the displays and enjoyed the ambience of a convention of people who loved dogs, I saw Jude Fielding now and then. He always seemed to be headed in the opposite direction, but we waved as we passed.

"You know him?" Lourdes asked. "Am I keeping you from meeting a friend?" He patted my hand. "I don't want to steal you away from anyone important."

"Just someone I was with yesterday." Impulsively I told him what Jude had said. "He recognized you as someone he'd met in passing. Just as I did."

"And he was nice?"

I thought a moment. "Very nice. He's a pilot. He flew some people here."

His response was to watch Jude disappear around a corner. "Another interest of mine. Flight."

"Then you'd enjoy meeting him."

"I'm sure you're right about that."

And so the morning went. I expected we'd spend the rest of the day together. We had lunch in the crowded café on one side of the building where Jude and I had had lunch the previous day. Then, with a dip of his head, Lourdes Jones said he had to leave. "Something has come up, I'm afraid. Something unexpected."

"I hope it's not a problem."

"No problem. I have an errand to run and unfortunately it can't wait. I apologize."

"That's alright. I should attend at least one seminar today."

We parted and I looked up the afternoon list of

seminars and chose one about sick puppies. When the session ended, I knew when to call the vet immediately as opposed to simply hugging a puppy and waiting a bit in case it was just lonely.

But as I left the seminar and wondered what to do with the remaining day I glanced up and saw Lourdes Jones. And Jude Fielding. They were together, wandering much as Lourdes and I had wandered that morning.

Then I remembered. I'd mentioned that Jude was a pilot and Lourdes had mentioned being interested in flight. I'd been dumped in favor of a guy who knew about planes, and I chuckled all the way to my next seminar, one with real, live dogs that showed off their well-trained selves to oohs and aahs from myself and everyone else in the room.

When I returned to my motel room that night, I wondered what would happen on the third and last day of the convention. So far, I'd met two very interesting men and had skipped more informative seminars than I'd attended.

The last day, though, wasn't to be so much for seminars and workshops as it was for speeches and the service dogs themselves roaming the halls with their trainers and showing what they could do and how well they could handle themselves. It promised to be a full and rather interesting day, with or without male companionship.

I'd never have guessed I'd spend that last day with both men, Lourdes Jones and Jude Fielding, though I could have guessed if I'd known what would happen when I arrived in the morning at the building with the huge, heavy, ornate doors that were difficult to open.

Lourdes Jones was at the entrance except this time he wasn't alone. Jude Fielding stood beside him as they talked animatedly but not so much so that Lourdes forgot to open the door for me.

I laughed as he swung it open and watched as he swept low in a bow and called me 'lovely lady' as he'd done the previous day, and I couldn't help but feel special. He might have been acting but it worked. I blushed and stopped and thanked him for being such a gentleman.

He took my hand and placed it on his arm as people did hundreds of years ago and steered us through the open doorway with Jude Fielding following and catching my attention with an expression that said it had already been arranged that the three of us would spend the day together.

Sometime during the day, Lourdes Jones repeated what he'd said that first time we spoke. "I'm impressed that so many people care about living beings of a different species. I think such people are special. In fact, I know they are." He looked straight at me. Through me. "People like you, Diedre Brown." Then he turned to Jude. "And also you, Jude Fielding."

Jude put up his hands in protest. "I don't train service dogs. I don't do anything with dogs or cats or any other species. I just fly planes."

"Jets, to be specific," Lourdes said. "Which is just as special in its own way as caring for a different species. Without pilots there'd be no flights and without flights how would anyone get around and see places other than where they were born and meet beings different from themselves?" He shook his head as if this was an astonishing fact. "They wouldn't, that's what.

So the way I see it, pilots and puppy caretakers are both special and I'm privileged to spend this day with the both of you."

Jude and I looked at each other over Lourdes' head and didn't know quite how to respond so we remained silent but the praise circled through my body and settled in some part of me that said it was a beautiful day that I'd remember forever and Lourdes was the reason.

Though, as I inspected the luscious, all-male Jude, I admitted that he was just as memorable though in a different way. I'd think about him a lot in the coming months. I knew I would. And I'd drool. Not that it would do any good. He'd have flown away in his jet, and I'd be back home doing other people's books and raising puppies.

As the day passed, both Jude and I realized something. We didn't speak about it in front of Lourdes but it was in the looks we passed between us over his head. The elderly, silver-haired man was playing matchmaker, and we were the couple he was trying in every way possible to get together.

When Lourdes went to get a refill of coffee, Jude's eyebrows rose and he said, "Do you suppose he does this often?"

"I hope not but if it's a habit of his I doubt anyone is insulted because he's such an all-around nice guy."

"I agree and if it's okay with you we can cater to his fantasy and pretend to be a couple for the remainder of the day."

"It will make him feel good." Jude nodded and it was agreed, and Jude took my hands in his as Lourdes returned and beamed beneficently.

We spent the rest of the day like that, hand in hand,

following Lourdes through the halls admiring the service dogs and their handlers. Lourdes clearly loved them as much as he enjoyed playing matchmaker. Several times he repeated what he'd said earlier. "I find it amazing and wonderful that so many people connect on so many levels with a species different than themselves." He shook his head in admiration. "It's absolutely wonderful."

We were sure that what Lourdes Jones did as the convention wound down was deliberate. We were in the cafe on the side of the building, and he'd insisted on treating us to a glass of iced tea. When he returned with three tall, frosted glassed and handed two of them to us, he took a long drink of his and said, "I do apologize but I must see to something. I hope you don't mind me cutting out a bit early. Do you?" We insisted we were fine with him leaving. "But you two mustn't separate just because I must go somewhere." He put his hands on ours and joined them together. "Because you make such a lovely couple."

Our eyes met as we silently agreed to go along with his matchmaking for a bit longer, so we left our hands together until we had to separate in order to drink our tea as Lourdes glowed with happiness because he'd created a loving couple. Us.

The tea was excellent. Beyond excellent. Our looks met still again with a silent agreement that Lourdes Jones knew his iced tea. We drank every last drop until Lourdes set his own empty glass on the table and left, turning for one last wave before disappearing.

Jude said it first. "I flew in a bunch of executives. I came to the convention because I had nothing better to do while waiting to fly them back." He raised his empty glass. It became a prism for the sunshine coming through the window and created a rainbow that danced on the nearby wall. "But it turned out to be much more." His eyes narrowed as he considered me. "And you and Lourdes Jones are the reasons. I'm glad I came. I'm glad I met Lourdes. And I'm glad I met you, Diedre Brown, even if we aren't quite the romantic duo Lourdes thinks we are."

I raised my glass too. It didn't catch the sunlight but our glasses clinked in a satisfying way as we toasted the convention and ourselves. "Me too. I'll remember these three days for a long time and the service dogs are only part of the reason."

Lourdes would have been pleased with Jude's next action. He leaned close and kissed me. It was a light kiss on the cheek but three days ago such an act would have been unthinkable. At the moment it was not only acceptable, it was perfect and I was sure Lourdes would have smiled.

CHAPTER 3

On the way out of the café we asked for refills of the wonderful iced tea to take with us. "Sugar or zero calorie sweetener?"

We chose sugar because that was most likely what Lourdes had chosen. The server took our glasses and gave us our tea in Styrofoam cups. We sipped it on the way out of the building. It was good but not the same as Lourdes had brought. Jude shrugged. "The server must be new."

"Hasn't yet learned the finer points of making iced tea like the one who made our first glasses." We laughed at the world of work that had both experienced workers and newbies and you got whichever was available at the moment. We pushed open the huge, heavy, ornate doors and left the convention building for the last time and headed for the parking lot.

I thought we both lingered longer than necessary as we reached a place where we'd go our separate ways, but it could have been my imagination. There was no reason Jude would be reluctant to see me go, though, as I found my car, I admitted to myself that I wished for a reason to prolong our leave taking. Because I wanted him to stay in my life longer. As long as possible. The attraction was that strong.

But he was a pilot, and I was a bookkeeper and our paths would never cross again and I might as well get used to that fact. So I turned away from him, climbed into my car and made the long drive home.

***

When I entered the house, I had turned into my own little corner of peace and tranquility, it felt odd. Not scary or uncomfortable. Not wrong, either. Not even close to wrong. The feeling wasn't anything I could define. But everything seemed different, and I somehow felt as if I wasn't the same person who'd left a few days earlier.

I stared at the mirror in the bathroom as I cleaned up after the drive and told myself that of course I wasn't the same person because look what had happened during those days. They'd been filled with two interesting men and a lot of wonderful service dogs. It would be strange if I wasn't changed.

I had a busy rest of the day. I caught up on as much work as possible, promised myself a busier next day of still more catch-up, and went to bed much later than usual. I expected to fall asleep instantly and I did.

But I didn't sleep well.

I had dreams.

Not nightmares because they weren't frightening or confusing. In fact, they were pleasant and very precise and that was odd because dreams aren't normally detailed. At least my dreams weren't. They tended to be blurry and indistinct.

But my dream that night was as detailed as if I was watching a rolodex display of pictures of a place I'd never been or read about or even seen in a movie, but the pictures were vivid down to sunlight filtering through tall, old-growth trees and flashing off ripples on a wind-ruffled lake.

It was a lovely place wherever it was. Somewhere up north, perhaps, because the trees were evergreens?

Though as to that, I decided when I awoke in the dark and went over my dream, many southern areas also have evergreens. But the lake had the crystal clarity typical of northern lakes so I thought that was where the dream place must be. And the dream had felt northern.

Except dreams aren't real and why was I thinking about mine as if it was? It was a dream, just a dream, and the only thing odd about it was that I remembered it so well the next morning. Every second of it. The blue and gray birds flying through the sky against fluffy white clouds. The doe and fawn drinking at the edge of the lake and then lingering a while before returning to the forest. I shook my head in puzzlement as I finished breakfast and turned on my computer to begin the day's work.

Then I stopped because someone called out. "Diedre." Someone in my house. Except, as I soon learned, there was no one there. I checked all the rooms and realized it must have been my imagination. So I shook my head, decided I had an overactive imagination, and went back to my work and concentrated on payroll.

But if it was my imagination why didn't it stop? Because it didn't. It kept calling my name. "Diedre." I knew it was imaginary but it continued. As the voice called again and then still again – okay it didn't call because it was imaginary, but it felt real -- I finally gave up getting anything accomplished and pushed the bookkeeping aside.

I closed my eyes and concentrated on listening because by then I'd decided it was potentially a real voice after all and someone was playing a very unfunny joke on me and if I listened hard enough, I might figure out who it was and deal with them severely. But no matter how hard I tried I couldn't recognize the person belonging to the voice.

As I listened intently, I realized it wasn't a normal voice, though precisely how it was abnormal I couldn't figure out. A computerized voice? Maybe but maybe not. An actor that was adept with foreign accents? Again, I couldn't know for sure.

In fact, no matter how hard I tried I couldn't pinpoint what about the voice was odd. Just that something was and that made it impossible for me to know who of all my acquaintances might be doing such an unwelcome thing.

The upshot of all that concentration on the voice meant I got nothing done that day and went to bed knowing I'd better get a good night's sleep because the next day I'd have two days' worth of work to do and I'd better get it done because a business was counting on me for their payroll.

But I didn't get much sleep that night either because once again I dreamed that same dream. Except this time there was an added element. Jude Fielding, the jet pilot from the convention, was in my dream, looking at me in a way he'd never done at the convention, rather in the way I'd wished he'd looked at me. Wanted him to look at me. Hoped he would. But he hadn't.

Darn! The man had definitely got to me if I was now including him in my dreams.

Then things got worse. In my dream he not only looked at me in that special man-woman way, he spoke in a husky, emotion filled voice. "Do you like the lake as much as I do?" In my dream I nodded, and his eyes crinkled in a way that made me stop breathing. "Then let's go for a swim because the water is crystal clear, though it might be a bit cold."

In my dream he dipped a hand in the lake and flicked drops of water that I caught with one hand, and he was right. It was perfect, though cool. And I pulled off my shirt to reveal a swimsuit beneath and headed for the water beside Jude who was doing the same.

What magic had the guy wrought on me at that convention that I not only dreamed of him, I'd inserted him into my other dreams and they were getting progressively more and more romantic. Pretty soon, in my dreams, we'd be making out. And more.

Fortunately, I woke up before our dream selves reached that point. I sat straight up in bed, threw the covers off, and stared into the darkness.

This was crazy.

I was crazy.

Then, in the middle of the night in my bed, I heard that voice again, the strange, unrecognizable voice that wasn't normal but I couldn't figure out how it was abnormal. But this time it only said one word. A different word than before. It said, "Come." Then it repeated that single word. "Come."

Then the voice faded away and I was suddenly cold and felt very alone in the house I'd always loved and felt comfortable in. I hugged myself and decided I'd better get myself straightened out if I didn't want to go insane and spend the rest of my life cowering in my own home.

I breathed deeply, lay back down, pulled the covers tight, and closed my eyes, determined to sleep without dreams for the rest of the night. That didn't happen. Instead, I spent the rest of the night dreaming that same dream. Over and over again and Jude Fielding was always a part of it.

Just before dawn, another element was added. Something new. Something different.

A light appeared deep in that dream forest that waxed and waned. If it disappeared entirely then it always reappeared. And never could I see what caused the light or exactly where in the forest it was located.

In the morning I woke up sweating and exhausted. This had to stop. So I went shopping and came home with every over-the-counter sleeping pill I could find. There was no doubt about it. I would sleep that night and I wouldn't dream.

Didn't happen. I still dreamed that same repetitious dream and every time Jude was in it, smiling at me and inviting me to join him to do something. Swim. Walk along a forest trail. Climb a hill and survey the wilderness. Always Jude. And the two of us were always doing something together.

In the morning I was more exhausted than the previous day but I dragged myself to my computer and worked without stopping until I was caught up. I sent the results to my clients and staggered to the couch where I dropped into the deep cushions and just stared at nothing.

As I lay there wondering if I'd sleep that night, I heard that unrecognizable voice that couldn't possibly exist but did. It repeated that single word. "Come."

It added my name and said, "Come, Diedre Brown."

Would it never leave me alone?

In total frustration, I picked up one of the couch pillows and threw it at the wall. The act felt so good that I repeated it with all the couch pillows and the ones on the chairs. When there were no more pillows to throw, I picked them up and carefully replaced them and wondered what I was thinking to have done such a stupid thing. What I was becoming. What was wrong with me. And I knew I had to fix me.

CHAPTER 4

The first item on my agenda to fix me was to see a doctor. I told him I was having trouble sleeping and could he prescribe something? He did and it worked for a night. Then it didn't work so I went back and said I needed a different prescription, and he referred me to a psychiatrist. That was the end of my seeking medical help. I refused to consider myself insane. At least I refused to admit it officially.

But I still had the dreams and when I checked myself in the mirror, I looked ten years older than the previous day. When I met another accountant, I often worked with, and we had lunch she said I looked like death warmed over. Later, at a business meeting a client said I looked overworked. Both silently backed away from me as if I had the plague.

I had to do something or I'd lose my business.

Then the voice scared me even more. When it spoke, it said more than it had ever said before. "Time is passing quickly, Diedre. There isn't much time left. I need you to come soon." The voice was gentle but I wasn't fooled, not even in the dream. It wasn't a suggestion. It was an order.

The next night the voice elaborated on the message. "You are one of two and you are both needed. I know you are both ready. So come, both of you. Come now."

The following day I tried to push away the terror that was beginning to engulf me. I concentrated fiercely on bookkeeping because I had a business to run that required my full and absolute attention. Numbers are like that. You'd better get them right.

But after two nights of being given orders by some unknown imaginary voice that couldn't possibly be real but seemed so, I admitted that the bookkeeping – and my life -- weren't going well. Something way more serious than anything I'd done so far was required.

I called a couple bookkeepers I knew and distributed my clients among them until such time as I could once more do a decent job. I said I was sure it would be soon but they insisted it wasn't a problem. "Take all the time you need. Get healthy." I hadn't told them what my health problem was, just that I had one and I was sure the friend I'd had lunch with had already spread the gossip about me. So, they weren't surprised.

Then something was added to the weirdness that was my life. But it wasn't just a new or different dream. It was strange in a new way but it had to be connected to the dreams somehow. I just didn't know how.

The new thing couldn't be easily described because it wasn't a voice. Nor was it a dream. Instead, it was pure emotion but it was an emotion so strong that it passed beyond mere emotions and became an elemental need, a compulsion so strong that it set my teeth on edge until my whole body thrummed with it.

As the hours passed with me going from one room to another in an attempt to get away from it and then out into the yard where I tried gardening without success, I realized I couldn't ignore it no matter what I did or how hard I tried. The new thing was a part of me no matter what I did, where I went, how hard I tried to push it away.

It would hound me whether I wished it or not and there was no way to shut it off because it was beyond mere communication. It was a compulsion, a need so deep in me and so basic, so elemental that it turned me inside out and took over my life, my every thought, my very being.

The compulsion told me to climb into my car and drive until I could feel in real life the coolness of the wind soughing through that richly green forest and the warmth of the sun on my body that I'd felt in the dream. It was so strong that I needed – absolutely *needed* -- to smell the piney woods and enjoy the ambiance of the tiny sand beach along the shore of the lake I'd never seen in real life and I also felt a desperate need to feel the water of that unknown lake on my body.

I needed to experience those things. I craved them as a starving person would crave sustenance. I believed my life depended on fulfilling the craving and the need grew stronger until it was a basic, gut-level, life-or-death compulsion so great that I absolutely had to experience those things, not just dream about them. I needed to *go* somewhere. To get in my car, leave my home, and just drive until I found them.

The compulsion told me to go north. To drive in a northerly direction and just keep driving until I found what I was looking for. It said I'd know it when I saw it. But of course, I wouldn't do that, or so I told myself. No sane person would let a mere dream dictate their life.

The compulsion and the imaginary voice behind it grew so strong, however, that my life fell apart. I couldn't sleep. I forgot to eat. I didn't bathe properly or shop for the necessities of daily life. I didn't clean my house. I didn't do any of the usual things people do. Eventually I knew I had to bring myself back to reality or I'd not survive.

I decided my first step in reclaiming my life would be to go shopping. Not just shopping, I decided, it would be a major shopping-as-therapy trip. It would get me out of the house and into the normal world and would begin with a leisurely meal at a restaurant with waitresses and a decent, healthy, gourmet meal. I'd be surrounded by normal people and would also get some nutrition into me.

It would work. It had to work.

I refused to think of the alternative.

So, I got in my car and managed to drive to the largest shopping mall in the city instead of north as the compulsion wanted me to do because there were restaurants in the mall.

North. It wanted me to go north because that was where I'd find the lake and the forest and the rest of the dream stuff. But I went south. I shook from head to toe with the effort of resisting the urge to go north and I was proud of myself as I looked through that mall for a decent restaurant where I'd begin my return to normalcy.

I was doing it. I was resisting the compulsion. But I saw no suitable restaurants in that mall so I left and went looking elsewhere.

I headed for an area I knew of with restaurants interspersed with motels that catered to travelers in addition to locals having lunch with coworkers and clients. I saw a nice-looking restaurant and started to turn into the parking lot.

I didn't. Instead, I drove past it because I suddenly couldn't turn the steering wheel to enter the parking lot. Couldn't. My muscles burned with effort but I couldn't do it. I swore at the compulsion but passed the restaurant anyway.

After that I passed two more restaurants without being able to turn into their parking lots either. Panic began to well up in me. Then, as I was beginning to believe my whole therapy type expedition would be a failure, I noticed a smallish family restaurant next to the first motel off the interstate. I decided to try one last time to turn into a restaurant parking lot. And I did.

I easily turned into their small parking lot and turned off the engine and climbed out of my car and looked at the restaurant. How was this cozy looking place different from the other restaurants I'd not been able to access? Why could I park here when I hadn't been able to park anywhere else?

But time was passing, so I pushed open the door and went into the restaurant proper, grabbed a menu from the stack on the counter and looked for a table. And stopped. Stared. And stared some more as my mouth dropped open in complete surprise as I saw the man from my dreams.

"Jude Fielding?"

He was a bit ahead, also holding a menu and looking for a table. He heard me. Turned. Saw me. Was as surprised to see me as I was to see him.

"Diedre Brown?"

"What are you doing in this part of the world?" His voice was weary, he was dressed casually and looked tired.

"What brought you here?" I countered with a

question of my own to give me time to come up with an answer to his question that wouldn't get me sent to the nearest asylum.

We sat at the same table without discussion. Of course, we did. We both showed up at the same restaurant in the middle of nowhere on the same day. An amazing coincidence.

"You seem tired," he said while not answering my question any more than I'd answered his as we stared at one another across the table like boxers seeking each other's weak spot, each wondering about the other while not answering the question we'd been asked.

I didn't want him to know what I'd been through even as I couldn't imagine why he was acting the same way I was. Cagey. Nor could I figure out why we both looked tired.

"Been busy flying executives around the world?" A semi-acceptable conversational gambit that went with his tired look.

"I'm on vacation."

"Because they've kept you so busy you need a break?"

He shook his head. "Actually, it's been slow. The last trip was for the service dog convention."

"And you're tired?" Surprise made me blurt it out. "From that one trip a while back?"

He slumped. "Not from work. It's –" He looked one way and then another. "It's complicated." He looked me over thoughtfully for a long time and changed the topic without answering. "So what's your excuse? Why are you tired and don't try to say you aren't. You look like you could sleep for a week."

I spoke without thinking. "I would if it wasn't for

the nightmares." I shook my head. "Not nightmares. Dreams, but the result is the same. Little sleep." That sounded reasonably normal. Everyone has dreams.

"You too?" Astonishment lit up his face. "I'm not the only one having dreams?" We stared at one another until he asked quietly, "If you don't mind my asking, just what are your dreams about?"

The waitress came for our order. We didn't notice until she cleared her throat and then we scrambled to order something from the menu. Anything. She left with identical orders because after I ordered the first thing on the menu, a rack of ribs, Jude said he wanted the same.

I was sure it was because he was too spooked to muster the ability to read the menu and not because he loved ribs. He hadn't even looked at the menu. He'd been too busy staring at me.

"So what are your dreams about?" He leaned way too casually over the table until hardly any space separated us but his eyes were intent, his nostrils flared, his words a little too carefully spoken, and he held me in thrall with a kind of magnetism as if we were connected by a rope – or a filament – or magic -- as he waited for my answer.

I squirmed. Looked over his shoulder. Wished I had a logical answer but I didn't. "Mostly I dream of a place."

The table was small, we were so close I could feel his breath stop and see his eyes widen at my words. He cleared his throat. "Your dream is of a lake in a forest." It wasn't a question. It was a statement of fact that he knew to be true. "It is. I know it is."

My hands moved restlessly on the table, this way

and that, unable to stay still though the rest of me couldn't move as I said, "And there's a light somewhere beyond where we are standing."

"You say 'we' because we are both in the dream." He took my hands in his own and we stared as our fingers laced together. "You and me." He exhaled slowly. "Am I right?"

I nodded. "Both of us. Sometimes swimming. Sometimes just being in the forest."

"Sometimes in a canoe? Do you ever see us in a canoe?"

I nodded again. "It's in one of the dreams. A birchbark canoe."

"And in one dream a doe and her fawn come to drink at the lake."

Words petered out and we simply stared at one another until the waitress returned with two orders of ribs. We waited until she left before continuing. "We are dreaming the same dream."

"Which is why we are both tired. The dreams won't let us sleep."

"And we were each told by some unseen, unknown voice that there are two of us." His voice was grim, and I nodded. "Though we aren't told what we are supposed to be two of." He pointed from himself to me and back again. "But it's clear to me now that we are the two the dreams are about. You and me."

He took a deep breath. I could see him decide to go for it, to make a fool of himself if necessary in order to know the extent of the truth that now lay between us like a dark pool of unknown depth. "It's because of those dreams that I took some vacation time and am headed north."

I was shocked. "You're following the compulsion?" I'd said it. I'd used the word. Compulsion. In saying it, I'd accepted that he, too, felt the need to go north. Just north. And he didn't argue with me. He thought of it the same way, I could see in his eyes that he did. What we both felt was a compulsion.

"It's the only way to regain a normal life. Find the origin of the dreams, look it in the eye, and then stare it into nothingness."

"I'm fighting it."

"Good luck with that."

I took an exploratory bite of the ribs. It was why I was there, after all, to have a normal experience in a normal restaurant. They might have been good ribs. I didn't know.

But the fact that I was there for lunch raised a question. Was I at this specific restaurant by choice or because at some level I'd been compelled to come here because it's where I'd meet Jude? I didn't ask Jude because I didn't have to. I knew the answer. We both did.

We ate for long moments in silence, looking at one another every so often and then looking away. Finally Jude put his silverware down, lay his hands on the table and waited until I looked at him and when that happened he dared me to look away. Then he said, simply, "Come with me. Let's find the source together."

The world stopped. I was sure other people in the restaurant continued with their meals and conversations and whatever else they were doing but I didn't hear any of it. Didn't see it. I only saw Jude's hands on the table, large and strong and male and the only voice I heard was his voice telling me to join him. "Are you saying I should just give up? Give in to it?"

"It's not giving up. It's finding out what this thing that's driving us insane is about. It's getting to the core of the thing. Going where it wants us to go so we can confront it and end it forever."

"What if it doesn't work out that way?"

"Then that's the chance we'll take." He took both of my hands in his and once again willed me not to look away. He was unafraid and was strong in his belief that this was the right thing to do. I wished I had his confidence. I held his hands tight and prayed for his strength to flow into me and tell me whether I should stay home or go with him.

"Okay." I said it. I committed to what he was doing. To joining him. "I'll come with you."

He squeezed my hands and then dropped them. Without his hands covering mine the room turned cool and fear pressed in on me once again.

I wanted to reach out and hold his hands and regain the strength I'd not realized until that moment he was giving me. But I didn't. Instead, I finished my meal as the world came back into focus slowly, sound by sound, person by person. When the waitress came to ask if we wanted dessert I was able to talk with her and tell her we didn't want dessert. Because we had something we had to do and had best get going. She understood.

We decided Jude would follow me home and wait while I contacted the bookkeepers who were helping with my clients to let them know I'd be gone for an uncertain period, and to pack practically my entire wardrobe because we didn't know where we'd end up and what the weather would be like. I also included my passport because Jude had brought his. When I was finally ready, the only things left in my closet were the dressy outfits I wore to business consults, weddings, and upscale lunches with friends.

When I was done, every suitcase I owned was full and every coat was in a pile and when they were added to Jude's luggage, the back of his SUV was packed with little space for anything more.

Then I just sat at the kitchen table and stared out the window at the yard I'd enjoyed ever since renting the house I called home with the fence that kept puppies safe and the picnic table I sat at whenever the weather was nice and the apple tree I'd sprayed with insecticide in the spring so I could enjoy apples in the autumn. Then I visited my next-door neighbor, the one who always kept my key when I went somewhere.

"How long will you be gone, dearie?"

"I don't know."

I was saved from further explanations when she glanced at Jude, who sat beside me with a closed expression. She tried to read him and failed and finally asked, "Family stuff?"

I nodded because that was as good a reason for an extended time away as any. "You do what you have to do, dearie. I'll watch your house and when you come back you come over and get your key and if you want to talk, I'll be here to listen."

I thanked her, grateful she'd made assumptions about why I was leaving and so didn't ask questions. Then I got in Jude's SUV, gave my rented but much-loved house a long, somber look, and turned forward as he pulled onto the street, and turned north. It was late afternoon by the time we got started so I didn't expect to go far that day. Not far enough to know where we were headed or even to get a good start.

The first part of the trip was easy. We wove through the streets of my small city until we reached the freeway. We pulled onto the north-bound half of the divided highway and Jude drove, keeping pace with traffic as I enjoyed the passing scenery because the release of stress that came with no longer fighting the compulsion and, instead, giving in to it was so great that it felt more like heading for a holiday weekend at one of the several tourist destinations north of the city than going on a wild goose chase for reasons unknown. I grinned and, glancing at Jude in the driver's seat, he grinned back. We were on an adventure.

Those tourist destinations we were headed towards consisted of resorts and motels near a state park with all the touristy fun things families could do on vacation. We drove until evening cast long shadows over the countryside though it was later than it appeared because it was summer, and the days were at peak length. As we reached the first motel, Jude started to turn in. And didn't. Instead, he passed it by, a frown marring his face.

"What's wrong?"

"I can't do it."

"The compulsion?" He nodded and fear started somewhere in my gut.

We passed three motels before we came to one he could turn into. It was much later and was full dark by the time we went inside. Jude asked if there were two rooms available and was told there were not but there was one we could rent.

Jude raised eyebrows asked if we could share a room and I nodded that we could. He turned back to the clerk and we were given that room. But when Jude gave the man his name, the clerk frowned. "I don't need this. You already have a room booked."

"No we don't." Jude was confused. We both were.

The clerk insisted we did and showed us the reservation. "It's paid for and everything."

"Who paid for it?

The clerk tried to find out. "It's a business credit card, that's all I know, from some place up north. It doesn't give the name of the business."

I wanted to leave. I was sure Jude did too. But we were there, we knew we'd not be able to stop anywhere else because the compulsion wouldn't let us and we were tired. So Jude accepted the room. One room and if we'd planned to share one anyway, we could share the one reserved for us. Surely there would be two beds because most motel rooms had two.

"Is there somewhere to eat nearby?"

The clerk said nothing would be open that late but the restaurant connected with the motel could provide sandwiches if that was okay with us. We said it was and were promised they'd be brought to our room.

We rolled our suitcases to the assigned room and went inside and simply sat on the one bed it held and knew we'd both sleep well even if we did have to share not only a room but a bed. It was huge, a king sized one, so it would be okay.

The sandwiches were filling, a meal, and we agreed that in the morning we'd find a grocery store and buy sandwich stuff and drinks and a cooler to keep them in. Just in case the compulsion wouldn't let us stop for meals.

"Surely whoever is behind it knows we must eat."

"We need to sleep, and it provided a motel room. So, it must also know we need to eat." He grinned suddenly and the day was brighter for it. "But either the person behind the compulsion is really cheap or it thinks we are married." He bounced on the one bed so I'd know what he was referring to..

I giggled, almost gagging on my sandwich. Soon Jude was laughing instead of just grinning and we finished the sandwiches and took turns showering in the adjoining bath and then we each laid out clothes for the next day and climbed into that huge bed.

Jude turned out the light. "Think we'll sleep?" Because we were sharing a bed? His next words said that wasn't what he was concerned about. "Will we have dreams?"

I thought about it. "If I have dreams and start tossing in my sleep, wake me, please."

"Same here."

And somehow, we fell asleep, and I hoped I'd not dream, that Jude's presence on the other side of that huge bed would provide a semblance of security that would let me sleep well and long.

No such luck. I did dream.

But it was different from any of my dreams so far. Instead of the lake, I dreamed of a road. Just a road. Not the black-topped freeway we'd driven that day, rather it was a narrow gravel road beneath old-growth trees that met overhead, giving travelers a cool, shaded path.

The trees were the same trees of the forest of my dreams and my dream self was eager to see where it led but the dream ended before I found out. The rest of the night was peaceful, and I awoke the next morning rested and refreshed for the first time since the dreams had entered my life. So perhaps Jude's presence had helped after all. Or perhaps it was because we were heading north and the pressure to resist was gone.

Th next morning we had breakfast in that restaurant attached to the motel. The compulsion let us take the time to eat. We were relieved. At least whatever was behind the compulsion understood that we'd not end up where it wanted us to be if we couldn't stay alive and eating was necessary for that, as were other normal, human actions. Like sleeping. And it let us shop for sandwich stuff that we tossed in the back of Jude's SUV on top of our luggage.

The fact that we could do these things meant the compulsion wasn't random. There was intelligence behind it. Possibly a computer program. More likely a person we couldn't imagine and couldn't picture because we had no idea what kind of person would do such a thing. *Could* do such a thing. Had the requisite ability and knowledge.

Huge power must be involved.

What kind of power did that person have and what kind of person was he? Was he a magician? A psychic? Or something beyond our ability to imagine?

Now you know a little about *Come to Me*. It'll be on Amazon and will be free with Kindle Unlimited. I hope you check it out and enjoy reading it.

GUARDING BRYNN

Florence Witkop

www.ingramcontent.com/pod-product-compliance
Lightning Source LLC
Chambersburg PA
CBHW060301310726
48976CB00007B/2164